FIVE FIRST DATES

ERIN MCCARTHY

Chapter 1

I SHOULD HAVE WORN A BRA.

That's all I could think in the hazy five seconds after I opened my apartment door, expecting to see my brother's best friend exactly how he'd appeared five years ago when I had last seen him. At eighteen Maddox Malone had been lanky and baby-faced, with soulful eyes like an owl, a serious and somewhat nerdy counterpart to my brother, Steven's boisterous swagger.

Then was then.

This was now.

Standing in front of me was not a boy fresh off of a Dungeons and Dragons game.

It was a man. A tall, muscular, brooding, tattooed everywhere hotter-than-hell bad boy who looked like he'd just stepped off his motorcycle. After taking his girlfriend against a wall and making her scream in pleasure.

His gaze swept over me.

My cheeks went hot with confusion at my very female reaction to him.

No, no, and no. He was practically family, what the heck was I thinking? I had to put this back on normal footing.

"Maddy!" I exclaimed, opening my arms to give him a hug.

I totally should have worn a bra.

Because he gave me a smile and put his arms around me (did I mention they were ridiculously muscular and tattooed?) and pulled me against his chest, which might have been mistaken for a cement wall it was so hard. I was absolutely stunned at the transformation. Someone back home should have warned me Maddox had morphed into a man that would make any woman drool. A text, a DM, a Snapchat, anything, people.

Hey, Savannah, Maddox got hot, wear a bra. A thick sweater. Baggy, not-sexy clothes.

I had the not-sexy down pat. I was coming off another night of total sleep deprivation, my hair in a messy bun, showering a distant memory. Was it yesterday? The day before? I wasn't sure. No bra because my nipples were killing me.

So why did I suddenly wish I looked thoroughly pulled together and adorable and desirable?

It had to be the lack of sleep. They say it does freakish things to your brain, causing hallucinations and everything. I don't know who they are but I was willing to buy it because I was absolutely exhausted and yet, was unnervingly attracted to Maddox.

"Hey, Savannah. It's good to see you. It's funny to hear you call me Maddy. I'm not a skinny kid anymore. I haven't heard that nickname in years."

Right. He definitely was not a kid.

My boobs were huge from nursing my six-month-old baby, Sully, and were pillowed against that massive wall of muscle Maddox called a chest. I felt trapped in his hold and I was flustered and awkward. I hadn't expected to feel either of those around a boy I'd known my entire life. But he wasn't a boy. Right. Not. A. Boy. My mind was blown but my body seemed to have figured it out more quickly.

I hadn't had sex since Sully was born (actually, seven months *before* he was born, so do the math) and my inner thighs chose now, of all freaking times, with my little brother's best friend, to decide it remembered how much fun the naked tango was.

Unnerved, I stepped back out of Maddox's embrace.

Only to see there were two little wet spots on the front of his T-shirt.

Holy hell. I had *leaked breast milk* on him.

I was a big advocate for nursing if you want to as a mother, that it's natural and bonding. I had really enjoyed it for the most part.

However.

Seeing the dampness on Maddox's black shirt had me wiping fabric, like I could make it dry with the magic of my fingertips, and babbling. "Oh! I'm so sorry. That hug... you squeezed me too tight and got me wet."

Maddox was eyeing me with amusement. His eyebrows shot up at my words. "I always wanted to do that," he drawled.

"Wait. What?" I stopped fussing with his shirt. "Do what?"

"Get you wet."

My mouth fell open. Who was this man and what had he done with quiet Maddy? "Was that a sex joke?" I asked, which was stupid. Of course, it was a sex joke, which I didn't need to point out.

I've always been known for blurting out my thoughts, but honestly, it had gotten way worse since Sully was born. Sleep deprivation had removed whatever filter I had to begin with.

He didn't seem to mind. "It was one hundred percent a sex joke."

"Maddy!" I smacked his arm, shocked. "I should punish you for that."

Now the corner of his mouth turned up in a dirty, mischievous smile. "Go for it."

What the actual hell was happening? Oh my God. I stepped back, tripping over the bench I had by the entrance to my apartment. "Come in."

Before all my neighbors heard this seemingly flirty conversation. I hadn't grown up in the city. I still had enough small-town girl in me that it bothered me to think my neighbors would know my business. I glanced back into my apartment out of instinct to make sure my son was okay, even though there was no way he could have moved from his pumpkin seat.

Still there, strapped in. I had plopped him in there when Maddox had buzzed from the front door downstairs. Sully's adorable moon face calmed me down. Geez, I'd made a cute baby.

I turned back to Maddox, reaching up to adjust my bun, which had gone off-kilter during the imprisoning hug from the Hulk. "Wow," I said to him. "I guess a lot has changed in five years."

Maddox had his suitcase and he set it down on the hardwood floors and closed my door. His gaze found Sully. "It sure has. So, let me meet the man of the hour."

I bent down and clicked the strap open and lifted my son out, giving him a big smile. "Hi, baby!"

He rewarded me with a huge gummy grin. I set him on my hip. "Meet Maddox, Uncle Steven's friend." I looked up at Maddox. "This is Sullivan Joseph Preston, but I call him Sully ninety-nine percent of the time."

Maddox took Sully's little hand and emulated shaking it. "Nice to meet you, Sully. We're going to be buddies."

They were. Maddox was going to be staying with us for the next eight weeks while he was working on a reality show at a tattoo shop. It had seemed like a fantastic arrangement for both of us when Steven had approached me with the idea. Maddox needed a place to stay. I needed a part-time nanny.

Now all I could think was that I needed to rethink everything about how I approached this situation because my baby brother's sweet and quiet scrawny best friend was now a walking female fantasy.

"You should change your T-shirt and I'll throw this one in the wash for you," I said. "It's going to start to smell sour." He may be a walking fantasy, but I wasn't. I was a new mom, and a bumbling one at that. I might be feeling inappropriate things, but there was no way he'd look at the hot mess I was right now and feel anything other than sympathy.

He probably had a girlfriend.

Feeling more stabilized and normal, I smiled at him. It had just been a shock to see him so filled out. Otherwise, it was no big deal. He was still Steven's best friend and like a brother to me. He'd practically grown up at our house. And this whole bad boy thing? So not my type.

I wanted a businessman who worked on Wall Street, wore a

suit, and would be happy to move to Connecticut in the not-so-distant future. I wanted a white picket fence and a garden and dinner parties. Book club.

Yep. No big deal.

Maddox reached behind his head with one hand and peeled his shirt off. My mouth went dry. He had tattoos everywhere, sprawled artistically across muscle after muscle. Six-pack? He had it. Biceps? For days.

I tried not to stare.

But there was just so much to look at.

I swallowed hard. "That's a lot of ink," I finally managed to say.

I COULDN'T TELL you exactly when I'd started having dirty thoughts about my best friend's sister, but it had been sometime around late middle school or early high school.

I'd waited a long-ass time for this moment, when Savannah finally saw me as a man, instead of an annoying little second brother, and you know what? It didn't fucking disappoint.

She was staring at my bare chest, her eyes wide.

"I like ink," I said simply.

"Apparently." Her finger came out like she was going to touch one of the images, but then she dropped her hand hastily. "You'll have to tell me what all of that means later." She ripped her gaze off my body and up to my face. "Did you eat anything? I can make dinner."

Savannah yanked the shirt bunched in my hand away and turned without waiting for my response. "I'll throw this in really quick. Sorry about that. Nursing has its unexpected complications."

It sure in the hell did. One unexpected complication was that I had found myself staring at her tits, which were absolutely huge. Porn star size. For a split second I'd had the dirtiest thoughts about what I could do with my cock between them, then I had realized she was nursing and I was a filthy bastard for wanting to touch every inch of a new mother.

Old habits were hard to break though, and I'd wanted Savannah for as long as I could remember.

She looked the same, only better. As a college student, Savannah had been a beautiful redhead, perfectly put together every time I'd seen her. That was her age of duck face selfies and sexy Halloween costumes, all which had fueled many a fantasy for my teen self. I'd rarely seen her without makeup and never like she was now, exhausted with her guard totally down. And yet, she was even more gorgeous than I had remembered. Yes, her hair was a mess in a pile on her head, and she had bruised skin under her eyes from lack of sleep, but she just looked beautiful to me, with her welcoming smile and offers to take care of me. When she was the one barely standing on her feet.

That's what had always appealed to me about her in addition to her beauty. Savannah was kind and generous and holy shit, I still felt all the same desire for her.

But just like when I was younger, Savannah, and her tits, were off-limits to me. According to Steve, that is. He'd known back in high school I had a thing for her and he'd made it clear he'd murder me if I so much as tried to touch his sister. The idea that I would then had been laughable. Savannah was the hot girl and I had been a nerd. Not the tape-on-his-glasses kind of nerd, but the dude who liked art, manga, comic books. I had been quiet and awkward and would have never had the balls to so much as hint to Savannah that I wanted to strip her naked, touch every inch of her gorgeous body, marry her, and give her everything she ever wanted.

Not that Steve had known the full extent of my crush. He'd thought I just wanted to bone his sister. Which I had. Still did. He hadn't understood that at sixteen I'd been convinced if I just hung on and grew up a little, Savannah would be my future.

Now here she was in front of me.

Everything had changed. And yet, at the same time, nothing.

I still wanted her.

"Don't fuss over me, Savannah. You're the one with a baby.

Point me to the washer and I'll throw the shirt in myself." I glanced around her apartment, curious to see how she lived. The place was small, which was no surprise for Brooklyn. I was just impressed she was able to support herself at all in New York.

The apartment was on the third floor of a townhouse-style building. The exterior had been a hodge-podge of different architectural styles and alleged improvements over the years, giving it a confused appearance. The interior had been left alone, the old thick woodwork intact, and the brick fireplace centered on the living room wall. Savannah's style was feminine, heavy on the pink with lots of throw pillows.

"It's no trouble," she said, not glancing back at me.

I followed her into the kitchen. It wasn't an open-concept apartment. The kitchen was a little galley hallway, cramped and narrow, but it did have a stackable washer and dryer at the end by the window. That would be a definite plus with a kid. When I was a kid and my mother had been working two, sometimes three jobs, I hated having to lug our dirty clothes to the laundromat on her day off.

"Let me hold the little guy at least." I moved in really close to Savannah because there was nowhere else to go in the small alley of a room. Her son was propped on her hip, his small fist bunched around the fabric of her shirt, causing the neck to pull down. The swell of Savannah's breast rose in a way that was hard to ignore, but I focused on the baby. He was a cute kid. Big blue eyes and full cheeks. He was watching me with a general suspicion.

I made faces at him and was rewarded with a brief smile. "He likes me."

Savannah turned and jumped a little. "Oh, wow, you're right on top of me."

I wished.

"Come here, Sullivan." I held my hands out.

"You're not wearing a shirt," Savannah said in protest.

"So?" I was entertained, I'm not going to lie. Savannah was unnerved by me being shirtless and I loved everything about that. "We need to get to know each other. Kids this age have separation anxiety when their mom leaves."

"I don't even know why I said that," she admitted, bending over with Sullivan and tossing my shirt in the washer. "Can you tell I pretty much haven't sleep in two weeks? I thought we'd reached a good spot. Sully was sleeping six hours straight but now he's been getting up constantly. I don't have a clue why." She stood back up and blew out a heavy breath. "Here."

She handed me the baby. Having spent my teen years surrounded by babies after my mother married my stepfather and had my four siblings back-to-back I was comfortable with her son. I held him up, mugged faces at him, and settled him against my chest. He didn't cry. He didn't necessarily look like he trusted me, but he didn't protest either. I figured that was a good start.

"Is he teething?" I asked. He was a little young for hard-core teething but that would explain the sleepless nights.

"What?" Savannah stared at me blankly.

"Teething," I repeated. Savannah looked exhausted and confused. "Listen, why don't you lie down and take a power nap?" I was pretty sure she'd started the washing machine without adding soap and now she was leaning on the wall like she needed the support to stay vertical.

"No, I'm fine," she protested. "You just got here. I want to help you settle in and we have a lot to talk about with the schedule, and how to take care of Sully. I want to hear about the tattoo shop."

"We can't do any of that if you're dead on your feet. Come here." I took Savannah's hand and drew her out of the kitchen.

She looked down at my hand like she couldn't process what was going on. "Where are we going?"

"To bed." It wasn't hard to find her bedroom. It was three feet down the hallway from the living room. It had one small window, a full bed, and Sullivan's crib. It looked like pre-baby Savannah had been organized with sorters, shelves, a shoe rack. But now it was cluttered with all the needs of a kid. Diapers, a monitor, stacks of clean clothes, and three pacifiers on the dresser.

"I shouldn't…" Savannah protested, even as she looked at her mattress with naked longing.

If only she'd look at me that way. Damn. She wanted that

bed, bad.

"Just get in bed." I put my hand on the small of her back and urged her forward.

"He just ate," she said, glancing back at me. "He shouldn't be hungry for a couple of hours. Wake me up after twenty minutes, okay? Not a minute longer."

"Sure. Of course. Trust me, we'll be fine." I eased back out of the room, pulling the door closed after me. "It's you and me, kid," I said to Sullivan.

He sneezed. Onto my bare chest.

That was a cool mist I could have done without. "Nice aim."

He gave me a toothless smile and a little squeak. His arms went up and down. He was a really cute kid. I had been expecting a ginger, like Savannah and Steve, but he looked more blond. So far, anyway. His hair at this point was more a promise than a reality. Just a few wispy strands.

"This is what we're going to do," I told him as I carried him back to the living room. "I'm getting a clean shirt out of my suitcase, then we're going to jump in the shower together while Mommy is sleeping. I want to wash the germs from riding the bus all day off of me. Not to mention your snot."

Sullivan probably neither understood nor cared, but I figured the sound of my voice might keep him calm and not crying. I wanted Savannah to get a decent nap. And no, I wasn't waking her up after twenty minutes. I was going to let her sleep until she woke up or until it was clear Sullivan needed a meal.

There was a play mat on the floor in the middle of the living room and I set Sullivan down on it so I could unzip my suitcase. My phone buzzed in my pocket, so I pulled it out. It was Steve.

"Hey, what's up?" I said, putting my phone on speaker.

"Hey, are you at Savannah's? She's not answering her phone."

I saw her phone was sitting on the coffee table. "I just got here a few minutes ago. I actually told her to go take a nap, so she's lying down. She looks exhausted, man."

"I told you. She's pretending she has it all together and I think she's full of shit."

"She seemed okay. Just tired." I pulled a clean T-shirt out of my suitcase.

"Who's watching the baby if she's sleeping?"

"Me, you dumbass. That's the whole reason I'm staying with her, remember?" I rolled my eyes in the direction of the phone, checked to make sure Sullivan hadn't somehow moved from the mat. I figured he was at the age where he could roll, but not crawl, but he still needed constant monitoring.

"You're staying with her because you can't afford to stay anywhere else."

That too. For me though that was secondary. I was really there because I wanted to spend time with Savannah and because I knew she needed help. "You're the one who said you wanted me to check in on her. Make up your mind."

For weeks, my best friend had been expressing concern for Savannah, along with irritation that the father of her baby had disappeared and she wasn't inclined to track him down and collect child support.

"No, you're right. I do want you to keep an eye on her. If it can't be me, at least it's you. She's almost your sister, too."

Right. My sister. Not.

Yes, I had affection for her. But my feelings were not familial at all.

"I'm on it. I'll make sure she's good while I'm here."

"Can you talk sense into her about the sperm donor? That guy needs to be held accountable. It's his kid too."

I couldn't dispute any of that. I also figured it was Savannah's decision, not ours, but I wasn't going to argue with Steve. I also didn't want to give a lot of thought to the man who'd knocked up Savannah. I preferred to think he didn't exist. That was selfish, though, and considering I had every intention of making Savannah mine, the asshole did need to be discussed at some point.

"That's not really my business but I'll see what she's thinking," I said mildly.

Steve knew nothing about my true intentions toward his sister. I was good at hiding my feelings. I couldn't let him know because he'd be pissed. He wouldn't believe me that my intentions were fucking honorable, which they were. I figured if I managed to get Savannah naked, he didn't ever need to know. It would be our dirty little secret. If I scored the ultimate prize—more than sex—he'd get over it and be fine.

We'd been friends too long for him to be truly angry.

Steve swore.

"Don't swear, you're on speaker," I told him. "Now I need to go. I'm watching this kid, remember?"

"Tell my sister to call me later."

"Sure. Talk to you later." I hit the button to end the call. Clean shirt in hand, I went and scooped Sullivan off the floor. "Time to hit the showers, kid."

I paused at the bedroom door. I risked opening it, easing it carefully so it wouldn't squeak. Savannah was sprawled out on top of the covers, legs scissored. Her hands were tucked up under her chin. She hadn't even taken her hair down or pulled the blanket over her. She was passed out cold. I was tempted to toss a blanket over her but I didn't want to disturb her. I also didn't want Sullivan to get any ideas about needing to crawl all over his mom right now, so I quietly pulled the door shut.

This was going to be harder than I'd thought. I'd come here hoping I'd be over it all. Over her. That I would see her and decide we were just friends, or honorary siblings, and my plans to slowly, surely, methodically make her see she wanted me as much as I wanted her would seem pointless.

That I'd enjoy her seeing me more as a man, but that'd be the end of it.

Yet not one single thing had changed in a decade.

I'd inked half my body, worked out and eaten protein like a beast, dated some really nice women I'd cared about.

Yet I was still half in love with Savannah and wanted to bury myself deep inside her.

"And I can't even take a cold shower," I told Sullivan, because my plan was to take him in the shower with me.

The baby's response was to kick me in the gut with his heel.

"Keep doing that," I told him. "I need someone to knock sense into me."

Chapter 2

I WOKE UP WITH A START, sitting up in panic. There was drool in the corner of my mouth. Why was I in bed? Where was my son?

I stumbled out of bed, heart racing.

I remembered almost immediately that Maddox had arrived and had told me to take a power nap. Right. Geez. I slowed down in the hallway, putting my hand onto my chest to take a deep breath and calm down. Sully was fine. He was with Maddox.

But when I went into the living room, they weren't there. I realized the bathroom door was closed and the shower was running. Hold on. If Maddox was in the shower, where was Sully? Was he lying on my bathroom floor, which I had to admit, hadn't been cleaned recently? The thought of my child rolling around on that cold, damp germ-riddled floor had me opening the bathroom door to rescue him.

Sully wasn't on the floor. He wasn't anywhere to be found.

My panic kicked into high gear again, and without hesitating, I ripped back the shower curtain to demand Maddox explain where the hell my child was. The words died on my tongue. Because Sully was in the shower with Maddox, looking pink and chubby and delighted, hand out in front of him to catch the water as he rested comfortably on Maddox's hip.

Maddox's naked hip.

Maddox, who didn't look pink and chubby and delighted.

Maddox, who looked like a hard, sexy-as-hell, bad boy.

His head was under the water, body turned toward me so Sullivan was out of the direct line of the stream. Which meant I could see every single full-frontal inch of Maddox. He was hard. Everywhere. Muscles on muscles, decorated with tattoos over a good fifty percent of his incredible body. Incredible and firm body.

I tried not to look at everything. I really tried. But my gaze seemed to have a life of its own and took a peek at his lower body.

My mouth went dry. My cheeks hot.

That was a big cock.

Inches from me.

"Hey, is everything okay?" he asked, pulling me out of my dumbfounded stupor.

I yanked my gaze back to his face, mortified.

"You didn't sleep very long," he said when I just stared at him. He didn't look even remotely uncomfortable with the fact that he was standing under a stream of hot water totally naked in front of me.

Finally, I pried my tongue off of the roof of my mouth. "I'm sorry, oh my God. I didn't mean to…" I gestured to his body. "I just woke up and I didn't know where Sully was and I freaked out. I'm not used to having help…" I trailed off, pressing my lips shut.

Maddox just gave me a grin. "Not a problem. I'm sorry, I didn't mean to scare you. I should have told you I wanted a shower."

Sully reached for me, bless his little heart. He saved me from further embarrassment.

"Grab a towel before you take him," Maddox said. "He's slippery." He looked down at Sully and bounced him on his hip a little. "Aren't you, little man?"

Now that my eyes were studiously focused above the waist, and I'd dragged my sex-deprived mind out of the gutter, I was amazed at how at ease Maddox was with my son. He'd been made to hold a baby, and as I reached for a towel, I felt a yearning for a father for Sully for the first time ever.

This was all really confusing, dangerous, and potentially disastrous.

I needed sleep and sex, clearly.

Towel in hand I got as close as was necessary to take Sully safely without touching any of Maddox's naked body. My cheeks were hot. "Maybe I can take a shower after you," I said. "I think I'm on day three without one."

"You could hop in now," he said. "There's room."

Maddox said it like it was totally normal. Like he wasn't naked in front of a woman who'd never seen him naked before. Like he had seen *me* naked before, which he most definitely hadn't. Like we were a couple with a baby and not old friends, if you could even really say that. It wasn't like I *knew* Maddox. We'd never talked about anything real. He'd just always been around our house with Steven.

This new dynamic was bizarre for me.

"Why are you teasing me?" I asked, genuinely curious. And again, no filter. "It was always the other way around. I teased you because I was older."

His eyebrows shot up as I took Sully from him and wrapped him fully in the towel. "Am I teasing you? Is that what I'm doing?"

"Well. Yes. Aren't you?"

He put his head under the water and ran his hand over it. A few water drops arched out and landed on my arm. So much wet skin. Everywhere, just skin and wet. Lord, I was losing it.

"I was flirting, not teasing. There is a difference."

That befuddled me. "Why?"

"Because you're an attractive woman and I'm a normal guy who likes to flirt with women. Or maybe I'm just being friendly."

I backed up, needing space. The room was warm and humid and I was having a very difficult time not looking where I shouldn't look. "This arrangement isn't going to work if you do that. Say suggestive things all the time."

"Why? It's not a big deal." Maddox stared at me with those dark eyes. Intently. "Is it?"

What the hell was he really asking me? I had no idea.

I was flustered and I took another step backward. "Maddy.

Stop. You're barely out of high school and I'm a mother. You're going to be my nanny. We have to be professional. Maybe that's not the right word, but you know what I mean. Friends who are helping each other. Platonic friends. Not *flirty*. You're like a little brother to me."

The look he gave me was smoldering. His nostrils flared. His shoulders tensed. He paused with the bottle of shampoo in his hand. "Sure," he said, his casual voice completely at odds with the intensity of his expression. "Whatever you want, Savannah. I promise not to flirt with you."

Then he grabbed the curtain and pulled it shut, blocking him from my view.

Good. Great. Perfect. Glad we had established boundaries. That was the way it needed to be.

I had no business behaving in any other way than as a big sister to Maddox.

So why did I feel so disappointed?

Because I didn't look at him and see a kid brother anymore. I hadn't known him in years and he was different now. It was terrifying.

I took my son out of the bathroom and to my bedroom to get him diapered and dressed.

Maybe it was time to start dating again. Over a year without a date or sex was clearly too long.

I was an eternal optimist. I believed in a happily ever after. I could watch romantic comedies for seventy-two hours straight. I loved *love*.

Unfortunately, I wasn't very good at it personally.

My friends all told me I was too quick to overlook red flags and to give people second chances. The first was probably accurate. The second I stood by. Everyone deserves a second chance. But my bullshit meter was definitely broken.

Sully's father had looked great on paper. A contracts lawyer. Apartment in SoHo. Wealthy parents who had given him a private school education in Manhattan. He'd said he was interested in a relationship. In leaving behind his playboy twenties and settling down into something "real" since he had turned thirty.

Apparently, an unplanned pregnancy had been too real.

I had expected him to be shocked and not entirely thrilled with the news. I had not expected him to be livid. When I had told him I was having the baby, he'd punched a hole in the wall, terrifying me. He'd said terrible things, accused me of entrapment.

No happily ever after.

Just me getting the hell out of there and vowing to stay the hell away from Adam. It was probably the first time I would not have given someone a second chance. Not that he'd wanted one, but my concern had shifted from my own personal feelings to concern for my unborn baby.

The maternal instinct was strong. Like the force.

I wanted no part of a father being around if he resented it.

Laying Sully on my bed, I rubbed his soft skin with the towel and felt my heart swell with love for him. He was perfection even if his sperm donor had been, well, not so great.

I hated to think of him as a dick. Even if he was one.

Moving quickly before Sully objected, I got a diaper on him and a clean onesie. Then little khakis and a blue sweater. The fact that they made khakis for six-month-old babies gave me a happiness I couldn't even express. Could anything on the planet be cuter?

I picked him up and gave him a belly kiss. "You look like a little man," I cooed to him.

"He looks like a Best Buy employee," Maddox said from the doorway. His expression was amused.

I frowned. Maddox was standing there in his towel. "What do you think he should wear, a skull and crossbones? He's six months old."

"That or maybe a puppy T-shirt or something. What you have on him now is what my grandfather wears to church."

Offended, I wanted to exit my bedroom, but he was blocking the door. "You have a lot of opinions for someone who isn't a parent. I'm the fashion expert, remember? I can handle dressing a baby. My baby."

He held his hands up, nearly giving me a heart attack when

his towel slipped. He grabbed it before it dropped to the floor. "Sorry. I was just teasing. I would never judge you on how you parent. I just thought since we're friends, we can be cool with each other."

That flustered me. I had really thought this was going to be a lot easier. More comfortable. But Maddox was confusing me. "I guess that's fair," I said, because I didn't know what else to say. "I did used to tease you a lot when you were a kid, like I said before."

He was leaning on the doorframe, showing no signs of moving or getting dressed or even putting the towel back in place. He was just holding it in front of his junk, but his hips were exposed.

"No, you didn't. Not really." His voice was soft. "I took a lot of crap from other kids for being the poor kid with the hot, young mom, but you weren't like that. You were nice to me, Savannah, and I appreciated it. More than you know."

My shoulders relaxed. I felt a warmth for him that was more familiar territory. Maddox had been a quiet kid, Steven his primary friend. I had felt sorry for him because he'd lived over a restaurant in downtown Stroudsburg while the rest of us in our school lived in suburban houses. His mother had been a waitress, very young, a MILF before the term had existed. Guys had always been catcalling her and flirting with her and she'd been sassy, flipping them off and hurtling wisecracks back.

She'd called Maddox "Weirdo" all the time. It had seemed to be an affectionate nickname, but not one I would have enjoyed.

"How is your mom?" I asked. "And your brother and sisters?"

He finally wrapped the towel around himself fully, tucking the edge. "She's good. She's freaking out about turning thirty-nine, but otherwise she's great."

Holy cow, his mother was only thirteen years older than me? That would have made her fifteen when he was born. Having been raising Sully on my own for six months at my age, I had a whole new respect for his mother.

"The kids are all mostly normal, mostly not assholes." There was warmth and pride in his voice. "Mike is great, too. I never thought I wanted a stepfather but he's an alright guy. He's the one who got me interested in ink. And motorcycles."

His stepfather owned an auto body shop back home and he'd seemed successful, moving Maddox and his mother into a colonial before they started producing children one after the other. They were a *cool* family, with artistic children, and yes, skull and crossbones on their clothes. In comparison, my family had been very traditional. My mother was a teacher, my father an accountant. There was a lot of khaki and beige in our house. I was comfortable with beige. I wanted a colonial in neutral paint colors someday.

I glanced at Maddox's chest. I couldn't help it. It was right in front of me. "I'll make some dinner while you get dressed and you can tell me all about your ink."

"Sounds like a plan. Here, give me the baby so you can do your thing in the kitchen." He reached out for Sully.

When he did, the knot on the towel gave way a second time and it pooled at his ankles. He didn't react at all to being fully naked.

He just took my son, saying, "I didn't mean to mock your threads, little man. It's not your fault your mom digs khakis."

He turned and walked down the hallway, ignoring the towel, and giving me a mouthwatering view of a very tight ass.

Note to self: Maddox was comfortable being naked.

I scooped up the abandoned towel and debated whether that was the world's greatest news or the worst.

I WASN'T TRYING to mess with Savannah. I really wasn't. But I was comfortable in my skin, and while I had long ago come to terms with the shitty moments of my childhood, I did appreciate that her whole family had been good to me. Maybe that had come off wrong though.

And okay, I wanted her to *want* me. I had to be honest about that.

She seemed unnerved though and I realized as we sat on the floor around her coffee table, which she'd set like a dinner table, that I needed to do exactly what she'd asked for—be her casual friend and nanny, nothing more right now. I had a lot at stake, and some of it had nothing to do with her.

"Tell me about the show," she said as she took a bite of grilled chicken.

She'd whipped together a salad and chicken. She'd also put on a bra, much to my disappointment.

Rebel Ink was the reason I was in New York City. "We're filming ten episodes, but it hasn't been picked up by anyone definitively. They're going to use the pilot to pitch it. All of the artists are under twenty-four, including the owner. It's partially scripted, and we're supposed to already know each other. We're implying we've all been working there a while, instead of hired for the show."

"Emphasis on youth, hmm." She glanced at Sullivan, who was sitting next to her, chewing on a stuffed animal. "That makes sense for Brooklyn. It's a cool opportunity. Are you nervous about being on camera?"

My whole life I felt like I'd been scrutinized. I shrugged. "No. That doesn't bother me. I think I'm going to have a harder time having to pretend to be pissed at people when they give us fake tension scenes. It's not my personality. But I really want this to work out, so I'll do whatever I have to."

"Request you be the flirt instead of the angry guy, then," she said. "Since you claim to be so good at it."

I gave her a smile. "I am charming as hell."

Savannah rolled her eyes. "What you are is hot. Girls are automatically going to respond to that."

Interesting. Hot, huh? I'd take that. Guess I wasn't so much a little brother to her, after all. That particular comment had annoyed me. I didn't appreciate anyone implying I was immature.

I'd never been immature. At five I'd been getting myself up with an alarm for kindergarten while my mother slept in after working late. My babysitter at night had been a woman who had been very sweet, but eighty-five years old. I'd fed, bathed, and entertained myself. As a teenager, I'd become a chauffeur and babysitter to four siblings. And I didn't resent one single thing about any of it. I was proud of my mother and me. I loved her and my siblings with all my fucking heart.

But don't tell me I'm a kid, and don't tell me how I feel.

Those were my two buttons and Savannah had inadvertently pushed one.

"So you think I'm hot? And here I thought you said I'm barely out of high school," I said. Then I gave her a smile so she wouldn't see how serious I was about that. "Doesn't matter what the show wants. I can only be me. They'll either be cool with it or not."

"It's a huge opportunity for you, though. You'll get exposure and future clients. You should play whatever character they want you to."

I stabbed a piece of romaine lettuce. "I'm going to try, but I'm not really that guy. It's going to be a challenge for me. I believe in being straightforward."

"What is your end goal? Are you hoping they'll pick up the show and you'll move here permanently?"

I shook my head. "I think the odds of that are small, but I guess it is a possibility. That would be amazing, obviously, but I want to be realistic. My thought was more that after the episodes air, people will recognize me as an artist and trust me. My plan is to take the money from the show and open my own shop in Stroudsburg. I want to be close to my family and I would prefer to run my own business."

"That sounds like a great plan. But if you wind up on the show for a few years, we're only ninety minutes from your family. It would be easy to see them. How old are all your siblings now?"

I pulled my phone out of my pocket and found a picture. It was me and the kids standing in front of Mike's shop. "This was right before I left." I pointed to my sister to the right of me. "Bianca is eleven now. She's a great student, changes her hair color weekly, and looks so much like my mom it's freaky."

"Definitely a cool girl," Savannah said, nodding. "Arms folded, head tilted, purple hair. She knows who she is."

"That is very accurate. This is Lillian." I tapped the screen to my sister, who was draped across my back, leaning on my shoulder, her hair covering half of her face. "She's ten. The most like me. Quiet, serious. Then this is my sister Kyle. My parents took a detour on the feminine names. I think they were thinking she'd be the last kid." Kyle was flashing deuces, legs apart, pretending to be tough. "She's eight. Then this little punk is Sebastian. He's six and fearless. It will be a miracle if they can keep him alive."

Savannah laughed. "Don't tell me that. That's my fear as a boy mom. That Sully will be more than I can handle. I wasn't a daring kid."

"Sully will probably be more chill. Sebastian is the youngest of five kids. He's fucking wild. It was a given."

"I like his Mohawk," she said. "And I see he has temporary tattoos." She pointed to my brother with his fists out, BAD BOI written on his knuckles.

I shook my head, laughing. "Bianca got hold of a Sharpie and did that. My mother was not thrilled."

Savannah was watching me, no longer looking at the photo. I closed my photos and turned to meet her gaze. "What?"

"I was just thinking that Sully is probably going to have a childhood like yours. An only child for years, then suddenly siblings. It's good to see how much you love your brother and sisters."

I didn't want to think about Savannah marrying some future guy. "You have no idea what is in store for you," I told her. "You could be married in six months."

She laughed, pushing chicken around on her plate. "That sounds ridiculous. Wonderful, but ridiculous."

"Wonderful?" I asked, my eyebrows shooting up. That was an interesting word choice.

"I like relationships," she said, her cheeks turning pink. Her fair complexion made it easy for her to blush. "I want to be married. I want to have inside jokes and Sunday morning snuggles and date nights. I know that's not a popular viewpoint to have now but it's true."

"I think there are a lot of people who want to be married." Me included. I'd never be the fall-on-a-different-woman-every-night guy. I wanted what my mom and Mike had, not the endless dates and lousy relationships my mother had before that. "Nothing wrong with knowing yourself."

"But I suck at choosing men. I fall for the lines, for the pretty face, for the promises. Every time. And they're always not very nice men."

"Is that what happened with Sully's father?" I asked, figuring it was as good of an opening as any.

She nodded and looked over at her son. "He said he wanted a serious relationship but I think he was just telling me what I wanted to hear. He was not happy about the pregnancy."

Reaching across the table, I covered Savannah's hand with my own. "His loss. Not yours."

"Sully's loss too."

That pissed me off on her behalf and the kid's and made me thread my fingers through hers to squeeze her hand. "No. Sully's gain. Nothing good comes out of having an asshole for a father popping in and out of his life. I don't know my biological father, and trust me, from what I've heard, it's better that way. No anger, no bad memories, no waiting for a dad to show up that never did. If a man doesn't want to be a father, good riddance."

She gave me a soft smile. "Thanks, Maddy. I mean Maddox. Sorry. I didn't mean to get so melancholy or tell you my sob story."

"You've got a lot going on and you're a great mom. Bottom line."

"Maybe I need an arranged marriage," she joked. "Let someone else pick a man for me. They couldn't do any worse than I have."

Interesting information. I wasn't sure if it was going to aid my cause in any way, but I thought it couldn't hurt it. "Maybe you just need to trust your gut more."

Or maybe she needed me to arrange a marriage for her.

To me.

Chapter 3

I STARED down at Maddox's hand entwined with mine. It was a strong hand, callused and covered in tattoos. It looked like brambles had wrapped themselves around his fingers. It was elaborate and beautiful, though dark.

"Did that hurt?" I asked, tapping my thumb onto his hand, both curious and to change the subject. I eased my hand out from his. I'd gotten a little too revealing with Maddox. What guy wants to listen to a woman talk about her romantic failures? I'd made myself sound totally thirsty for a man and that was a little embarrassing.

Maddox gave me a slow smile. "What's a little pain in the pursuit of pleasure? It's clearly not intolerable or I wouldn't keep doing it."

That basically summed up my dating life. "I'd like to see your portfolio sometime."

"Sure. But what about you? Aside from this guy, what's new? How's work going?"

I glanced over at Sully, giving him a smile. "It's good, honestly. I'm really fortunate I can work at home, though I have to admit I'm a little behind right now. It's hard to be posting videos about looking cute for a trip to Barcelona when I'm sitting in my apartment in Brooklyn in yoga pants."

"How does that work? Does the site give you assignments or is it more freelance?"

I'd been at Snap, a lifestyle and fashion site and video channel, for almost three years. "I have standard features that are expected to be turned in on certain days of the month, but there are also articles or topics that are assigned to me. I used to go into the office a couple of days a week, because I loved the energy and vibe of being with my co-workers, but now with Sully it's perfect to be able to work at home."

"So how can I help you, make life easier while I'm here? You're doing me a huge favor letting me invade your space and crash on your couch. What do you need from me?"

More than I'd initially thought. Sex immediately came to mind and I was shocked and annoyed with myself. "You're doing me a favor too, you know. It's mutually beneficial."

Maddox took a sip of water. "Call it what you want but use me, Savannah. Seriously. That's what I'm here for."

Use him. Oh, I'd like to use him all right. I swallowed, hard. My cheeks felt hot. But I was determined to read nothing into that. I didn't think he'd meant it as an innuendo. His face looked too casual.

"I'll show you around the apartment and go over with Sully's routine with you. Mostly I just need backup after work and maybe a night or two a week for the chance to escape the apartment by myself."

He nodded. "I can handle that."

I bit my lip sheepishly. "Any chance you can watch Sully tonight?" I asked. "My girlfriends are all meeting up for a drink. It wouldn't be long, I swear."

"Of course."

Maddox didn't look offended or annoyed. He looked very neutral.

But I instantly felt guilty. "But you just got here and I feel like I'm already taking advantage of you."

He shook his head. "No, you're not. That's what I'm here for, to watch Sully. Go and have fun. We'll be fine, I promise. A little guy time, hanging out, watching Thursday night football. Are you going into the city or staying in Brooklyn?"

"Brooklyn. My friend Leah complained but I told her I couldn't go out unless we stayed close to my apartment. She grumbled, but agreed."

"Perfect." Maddox rose from the table and took both my plate and his and headed to the kitchen. "Will Sully take a bottle if he gets hungry?"

"Yes. There's milk in the fridge." I stood up and lifted Sully onto my hip. It was really, freaking nice to have help for a change. "Thanks, Maddy."

He glanced back, expression unreadable. "My pleasure."

His voice was like fingers stroking over my body. Yep. It was definitely time to have my girlfriends help with Operation Four First Dates.

They were going to love saving me from myself.

"HOW IS THE MANNY?" my friend Leah asked me as she flagged down the waitress. Leah had the glow of a woman recently in love and it was *adorable*.

She and Grant Caldwell were super new, but she was head over heels for him, and he was even more so for her. The man was giving up a penthouse apartment to live with her. After a whirlwind romance, they were now engaged. Could it get any more romantic? I don't think so. Hashtag nope.

Wishing desperately I could order a glass of wine, I eyed each of my best friends at the round table with enough of a pause to create the drama I wanted. Current events needed to be dissected and it would be fantastic to have a crisp chardonnay but nursing made that impossible.

Isla's eyebrows went up. "Someone please tell me that Savannah hasn't fallen in love with the male nanny in the course of one day because I will lose my shit. I mean, legitimately lose my shit."

I smacked her arm. "Stop. You make me sound nuts. I have not fallen in love in one day."

"If the glass shoe fits."

Isla was a cynic. She called herself a realist but let's be honest. She was sinking into Bitterville whether she wanted to admit it or not. I totally worried that one day she would wake up miserable and realize she'd wasted a decade hating people in general, men specifically.

"Don't make this about you," I told her, sitting up a little straighter. My jeans were gutting into my post-baby gut. I felt lucky that only five pounds were being stubborn and sticking around, but they were all in my midsection. When I spent every day wearing yoga pants it was easier to ignore, but maybe it was time to go shopping for a size up and spare myself this minor torture.

"About me?" Isla snorted. "How is that?"

"About your determination to hate on relationships. I didn't even get to say one word and you went straight to love. Clearly you're obsessed with it." This was a thing Isla and I did. We bantered about what ultimately was both our favorite topic, just from different perspectives.

"Here we go," Felicia said, her British accent making it sound particularly clipped.

"Tell us about the nanny," Dakota said, wearing a bodysuit that plunged in the middle to the navel.

It was a bold choice for a Thursday night, but that was Dakota. She was six feet tall and had legs that came up to my armpits. She wasn't much for drama, except when it came to her style. She embraced her height and dancer's figure.

"The last time I saw Maddox he was eighteen," I told them, pausing to take a sip of water. Anymore I never had anything to contribute to conversations about dating, so I wanted to draw out the impact. "He was skinny, quiet, into Dungeons and Dragons."

"Those guys always have huge dicks," Dakota said.

She wasn't wrong in Maddox's case. My cheeks burned as I pictured him in the shower, water running down those abs and right over a very impressive cock...

"I think that's off-topic," Felicia said.

"Not if you look at Savannah's face," Leah said, sounding very gleeful.

"I didn't have sex with him," I said, pointing a finger at Isla. "So don't start reprimanding me. But yes, his dick is impressive and I know that because he told me to take a nap and when I woke up Sully was gone. In my mom panic I barged in on him in the shower."

"Where was the baby?" Felicia asked.

"In the shower with him." I put my hands on my cheeks. "Girls. Maddox is big and muscular and tattooed *everywhere*."

"Everywhere?" Dakota asked. "What's tattooed on his dick? I always wondered how they do that. I mean, depending on whether you're hard or limp the art is going to look different."

That momentarily distracted me. I wasn't sure I could jump on a tattooed dick. Not that I was jumping on Maddox's. But I thought it might be a little unnerving. "What? No. His you-know is not tattooed. But a lot of the rest of him is and he's like this bad boy and it was shocking. I mean, I thought of him as a kid brother."

"And now you don't?" Leah looked around. "Where the hell is the waitress? It took me a fucking hour and a half to get here on the train. I want a glass of wine."

"Have Grant's driver pick you up," Isla said with a smirk.

"Ew. Don't be weird."

"It's not weird for your billionaire fiancé to take care of you," I reassured her.

"It's even weirder when you put it like that."

"I would let my billionaire fiancé send a car for me."

"You would let a prisoner put you on his visitor list," Isla said.

That made me laugh. "No, I would not. But anyway, back to my story, thank you very much. I saw Maddox and he's all man and flirty and cute with my son and I cannot, under any circumstances, go there. So I think I need to start dating again. I need you all to pick out my dates for me, because we all know I can't be trusted not to find the biggest douchebags ever."

"That's a lot to unwrap," Felicia said. "Can we start back at the beginning? So you're attracted to Maddox the manny?"

I nodded. My mouth practically watered. "I opened the door and I actually got *flustered*. Like, my basement flooded, if you know what I mean. I didn't even know I could get turned on anymore. But now I know I can, so it's clearly time to start dating."

"I feel there are some leaps in logic there," Felicia said. "One, why can't you date the nanny? Two, why do you need to date? Can't you just find a hookup?"

I eyed her. "It's like you don't even know me at all. I don't do casual sex. I don't even know how to do casual sex. I've tried and I've ended up spending six days straight in the Caribbean with the guy who was supposed to be a one-night stand!"

"Oh, God," Isla said, shaking her head. "I remember what will forever be known as the Dante Debacle."

"I need to date, old-school. Find a guy to be in a relationship with, at least for awhile. Have some nice sex, and settle in for a couple of years." If not forever. But they'd protest miserably if I said that out loud.

"What about the nanny?" Dakota asked. "Since he's hung."

"Are you crazy?" Leah asked. "She just said she can't do friends with benefits. We all know that is one hundred percent true. She cannot have a man living with her for two months, watching her baby, while she complicates the hell out of it by falling in love with him."

That made me protest. "I wouldn't fall in love with him!"

The waitress finally appeared and all conversation ground to a halt so Leah could get her wine order in first. Dakota ordered a bourbon on the rocks, which made my throat burn just thinking about. Felicia got a martini and Isla a craft beer. I felt sorry for myself as I ordered an iced tea.

As soon as the waitress left, Dakota said, "Wait. So, are we one hundred percent sure she can't have sex with the nanny? I mean, how convenient. *Hey, I want to bang tonight and you're five feet away. Yay.* It sounds awesome to me."

"He's my little brother's best friend," I said. "Not only does that make him off-limits, that makes him like twenty-three years old. Maybe twenty-four, tops, I can't remember when his birthday is."

"Oh, you're worried he'll pop off too soon since he's young and uber horny? Fair enough," she said.

I should have known this conversation would get away from me. "No! I mean, I never thought about that. But I doubt it." I pictured Maddox's intense stare. "You don't understand. Even as a kid, his concentration was crazy. He's a tattoo artist. He obviously has to be focused. No. I think he's probably the kind of guy who just draws it out on and on while you slowly go crazy with the intensity of it…"

Damn it. I could feel myself getting wet just thinking like that. I was wet. In a bar. Thinking about Maddox. If I had told my twenty-year-old self this would be the future, I would have laughed hysterically. The waitress put my drink down and I gulped half the iced tea in one sip. I was burning up from the inside out.

"Let's start with buying a vibrator," Felicia said. "Because I think you're a wee bit undersexed right now."

"Do you have a picture of him?" Leah asked. "I'm really curious what this guy looks like given how you're practically drooling."

"I bet I can find his Instagram." I pulled my phone out and scrolled through my apps. I should have done this before he showed up on my doorstep because at least I would have been mentally prepared. There it was. Primarily pictures of tattoos he'd done on other people. But there was one of him leaning against his motorcycle, arms crossed over his chest, expression brooding.

I passed the phone to Leah across the table. "Here he is."

"Holy fuck," Leah said as she looked at the screen. "He's so not your type."

"I know, right?"

She passed the phone around the table. One by one they exclaimed over the hotness of Maddox.

"If you're going to shatter stereotypes by having a male nanny, this is the way to do it," Isla said. "He's straight out of Breaking Bad."

"Can I have sex with him?" Dakota asked. "Since you can't for reasons I still don't understand."

"No!" I knew she was joking but it still irritated me.

"Don't tease her. She's in crisis," Felicia said. "Okay, so I'm following this better now. The solution is to date other men so you don't shag your nanny?"

"No. The solution is to date so I can have an orgasm and someone to spend Friday nights with. But I don't trust myself to pick guys out on an app or even in person. So here's what I'm proposing. Each of you picks a guy for me."

"This is the best thing I've ever heard," Dakota said. "You're telling me I can pick anyone?"

"Anyone that would be a good fit for me." I felt the first flutter of nerves over my seemingly brilliant idea. She looked downright gleeful.

"Anyone that I think would be a good fit for you, correct? Not *your* idea of a good fit. Because you've already dated every white suit-wearing prick in all five boroughs."

I opened my mouth to protest, then realized I had exactly zero leg to stand on. She was right. I was a prick magnet. The whole point of this exercise was to break away from the patterns that had resulted in nothing but heartbreak. If I always was drawn to the exact same type of guy, wasn't the outcome going to be the same?

"Yes. You can choose whoever you think would be a good fit for me. Not a fit for you. A fit for me."

"This is gold," Dakota said. "I have at least five guys at work that I'm mentally considering right now."

Dakota danced in music videos and for the pro football dance team. I was intrigued by who she might come up with. Me with a rapper? It boggled the mind and yet was kind of exciting. The whole point was new possibilities.

"Can we use an app?" Felicia said. "You know I've become a recluse since Sam and I split. I know no one in person to set you up with and I definitely want in on this."

Felicia had been dating older, wealthy men, being whisked away on vacations until she'd had a horrendous breakup. Now she hadn't dated in close to a year, and seemed to have lost her confidence entirely. She spent most of her time in her apartment, working. Maybe this wouldn't just help me. Maybe Felicia would join an app herself and get back out there. "Yes. Download an app if you don't have it already and I will give you my login. You can pretend to be me."

"That is a power that must be wielded responsibly," Isla said. "But I swear, you can trust me. I don't know about these other bitches, but I promise I won't muck around in your account."

"I trust all of you." I did. Implicitly. "That's why I'm doing this."

"I'm going to put feelers out with Grant's cousin," Leah said. "He's the CEO of a hotel chain."

"Sold," I said, grinning. This was going to be fun.

If I was going out on hot dates with four totally different curated men, obviously, I was going to forget all about Maddox and how he looked naked.

"You're getting your dream, aren't you?" Isla asked, expression amused. "It's your own real life rom-com."

"It is!" I said, eyes widening. I hadn't thought about that, but she was so right. "This is going to be epic."

"It's going to be something," she agreed.

Out of our squad Isla and I were the most different but I would argue the closest. She got me fully and I got her too. I knew things about her past the other girls didn't. And she knew my love of the romantic comedy bordered on extreme.

I raised my iced tea. "To four first dates."

They all raised their glasses.

"To having sex," Dakota said.

"To the rom-com," Leah chimed in.

"To having man candy living in your apartment," Felicia said.

I looked at Isla expectantly when she didn't offer her own toast. "Well? You have to say something too."

Isla tapped her glass onto mine. "To living close to the train station and reasonably priced poke bowls."

"Ugh! You're the worst," I told her.

She laughed. "Just keeping it real."

"I don't want *real*," I protested. "I want love."

Isla sipped her beer. "Yeah. And that's the problem."

"I refuse to let you ruin this," I told her. "I'm going to have fun and you can't stop me."

She held up her hands. "I'm not standing in your way." She lifted her glass again. "To Savannah's adventures in dating. How's that?"

"Better." I sipped my iced tea and felt confident in a matter of a few weeks I could be having sex again.

RIPPED OUT OF SLEEP, I immediately realized what had woken me up. A baby crying.

Savannah's baby crying.

Lying on her couch under a blanket I stayed there for a minute, eyes still closed, gauging the level and volume of his crying to see how realistic it might be that he'd settle down quickly and I could fall back asleep.

It didn't sound promising.

It was way beyond whimpering or fussiness. It was hard, sharp crying that was growing in sound and intensity. It was swelling to full-on wailing. Nope. That kid was not going back down any time soon.

Prying my eyes open, I let them adjust to the dark and threw the blanket off of me. I was sleeping in sweatpants without a shirt. Fumbling on the end table, I found my phone. 2:24 a.m. Savannah had been true to her word. She hadn't even been gone meeting up with her friends for a full two hours. Sullivan had been fine for me. We'd played and then he sat tucked in the crook of my arm while we watched the Eagles kick ass on Thursday night football.

He hadn't even made a peep about needing to eat. Savannah had gotten home at nine, nursed him, then he'd been out like a light. So had she. She'd stayed up to talk to me for about fifteen minutes, then had yawned so many times I'd let her off the hook and sent her to bed.

Now little man was screaming bloody murder.

I went down the hallway and knocked on the door.

Savannah yanked it open a second later. The nightlight in her bedroom cast a glow onto her and the baby. "I'm so sorry, Maddox," she said, juggling Sully up and down. "I know tomorrow is your first day at the shop. I don't know what's wrong with him."

"Don't worry about me," I told her, sincerely. I wasn't someone who needed a ton of sleep. "I just wanted to see if I can do anything to help."

"I don't know what to do. He's been changed, fed, he doesn't have a fever."

She looked so flustered, I reached out and squeezed her shoulder. "Hey, it's okay. Sometimes babies just cry."

"It's the worst sound in the world," she said, blowing her hair out of her eyes. "It hurts my heart that he's suffering."

I eyed Sully. His face was beet red from his exertions and he had fat, wet tears clinging to his eyelashes and rolling down his cheeks. His head was lolling back and he had fists tightly gripping Savannah's loose T-shirt. A bubble formed in his mouth. The kid was either pissed or in pain. That was clear.

"Does he sound angry to you or in pain?"

"I don't know!" She bit her lip.

"Yes, you do. You know your baby. Just take a deep breath and relax." I touched Sully's arm. "What are you trying to tell Mommy, little man?"

Savannah smoothed his wispy hair back and stared at her son. "Why would he be angry? He was sleeping. It has to be pain, then. Maybe it's gas. I shouldn't have eaten broccoli. They say it's hard to digest."

Her tone had changed from panic to guilt. "Here." I reached out for him. "Let me burp him. Maybe that will knock something loose."

Savannah was flustered enough that she handed Sully to me without protesting. "Do you know how to burp a baby?" she asked.

I scoffed. "Are you kidding? I'm the king of burping babies." I lifted a hand and showed her. "Big palms, loads of experience."

Putting Sully over my shoulder I massaged his back, then patted firmly but gently. The first few taps yielded no results but then he let one rip. I felt warm spit-up roll down my bare skin. Damn. I ignored it and continued to massage his back as the shrill crying settled down into wet hiccups and shuddering.

"I think that did it," Savannah said, sounding relieved. "Thanks, Maddox. Here, let me settle him down so you can go back to sleep."

"I think he's falling asleep already," I said, as Sully started to sniffle. "He wore himself out. Let's sit for a minute until we're sure he's out, then I'll transfer him to his crib. I know how dicey the transfer is."

Savannah gave a soft laugh. "It's like dismantling a bomb."

I sat down on her bed and leaned against the headboard, making sure Sullivan was comfortable and had plenty of space and air. I lifted my legs onto the mattress and raised my knees. Savannah sat down next to me. She gave a sigh as she leaned back, pulling the blanket over her feet.

"You have fun with your friends?" I asked, keeping my voice low.

She nodded. "Thanks again for watching the baby." She reached out and ran her finger lightly over Sully's leg, covered in a soft pajama bottom.

Watching her, seeing her expression of love, was fucking with my resolve to let her dictate the boundaries of our relationship. I didn't think she had any idea how beautiful she was, inside and out.

"That's what I'm here for," I said. Sullivan's weight grew heavier as he relaxed. It felt like a huge achievement to calm him down, and I had to admit, I was feeling proud of that fact. "So are your girlfriends all single?" I asked, just trying to make conversation.

"Three out of four are single," she said. "Why, do you want an introduction?"

"No, of course not. I was just curious. Wondering what dating in New York is like."

"Leah has a new relationship and she's insanely happy. Isla doesn't date. Felicia is something of a recluse in recent months. And Dakota is a wild child. It's hard to tie her down." Savannah turned slightly toward me. "Why isn't my brother dating anyone? Or is he? He won't tell me anything."

I wasn't going to give up Steve's secrets but I could give her an abridged version of the truth. "Steve dates lots of girls. Just not one in particular."

She made a sound, like she didn't like the idea her brother was potentially a manwhore, which he was. I had no opinion on what my buddy did or with who. He took home a steady stream of women who were perfectly happy to have sex with him and nothing more, so I figured it was all good. Steve wasn't ready or interested in a relationship and was just having fun.

"And you?" she asked.

"That's not my style. I'm not a casual sex kind of guy. I like to settle in and get to know a woman, and when we have sex, I want it to be about her, about us, not some routine of moves I use on everyone."

"What do you mean?"

"When you have a hookup, you go in doing what you normally do, right? It's a standard set of steps. When you know someone, when you've been burning for them, when you look at them and want them so much your cock is aching, you do it for *them.* Every kiss, every touch, every lick, is based on what you know about them. What they like. What they crave. How do you do that with a stranger? You don't. It's based on what you want."

Her eyes were wide. "Oh. I see what you mean," she whispered. "I don't like casual sex either. But I'm not good at reading men. I always think they want a relationship when they don't."

"That's because you're a nice person."

"It's because I'm an idiot who thinks romantic comedies should be real life."

Good information to have. "What is your favorite romantic comedy movie?"

"I can't pick just one. Ten Things I Hate About You is up there. The Proposal. Leap Year. Always Be My Maybe. There are just too many."

I hadn't seen any of those. We were more of a horror movie kind of family. "What is it that makes those special to you?"

"I think it's the idea that we basically overcomplicate love and relationships. It's there, all around us. If we want it. That's the message." Savannah touched her son's foot again. "Not that it's worked for me. Which is why I told my friends tonight they each have the authority to set me up on a first date."

Yeah, fuck that. But I kept my expression neutral. "With whoever they want?"

"Yes. Because they know me and should be able to gauge who I can click with. Do you mind watching Sullivan? It's only four dates, but you know, the goal is one of those will be second-date-worthy."

Watch her baby while she went out and tried to find Mr. Right? That sounded like fucking hell. But I didn't have a choice. If I said no, she'd think I was a total dick. So I would bide my time and assume her dates were going to suck.

All while I showed her that I could be her happy ending.

"I don't mind. I just have one condition."

Her gaze lifted to meet mine. "What?"

"I get to pick your fifth first date."

She looked confused. "You want to set me up with someone too?"

I nodded. "Yes. I've known you longer than all your New York friends."

"Yeah, but, it's not like you know what I like."

It wasn't a matter of what she wanted. It was what she needed.

"You can tell me what you like in a guy. Come on, what's the risk? It's just a first date."

With me.

In the dim room, she gave a soft laugh, her expression amused. "Sure, why not? The whole point is statistics, right?"

"I thought the whole point was finding forever," I told her, my hand cupping Sully's body against my chest.

Savannah's mouth fell open softly and almost imperceptibly she glanced at my mouth, like she wanted to kiss me. Like the intimacy of a dark bedroom, a warm bed, and a sleeping baby had made her see me in a different light.

Or maybe I was reading more into it than I should.

I let my gaze drop to her lips.

She reared back, like she'd been shocked. She twisted the ends of her red hair and cleared her throat. "Why don't you try to put the baby back in his crib?" she said. "You need to get some sleep."

I did what she suggested without a word. Sullivan was worn out and when I eased him into his crib he didn't react at all. I drew the blanket over his legs and stood back up. Savannah hadn't moved from the bed. She'd pulled the comforter up over her and was clutching it to her chest, as if to protect her.

I rubbed the back of my head and padded toward the door. "Goodnight, Savannah."

"Goodnight, Maddox."

I closed the door behind me and stood there for a minute, listening. For what, I had no idea. After a minute, I went back to the couch, where I lay awake for an hour, cock hard, wishing I was in her bed, inside her.

I punched the pillow. "Not helpful, asshole," I murmured out loud.

Chapter 4

"ARE YOU EVEN LISTENING?" Xander asked me, his nose wrinkling as he stared at me via Skype.

I wasn't. "Of course, I'm listening. Best Holiday Outfits for under fifty dollars. I'm on it." I wasn't. Not really. It wasn't a hard assignment. I could do it in two hours. Normally, I jumped on something easy like that as a way to round out the afternoon and feel accomplished.

But I sat at my desk in my living room, gaze going back to the couch where Maddox had carefully folded his blanket and set his pillow on top of it. There had been something very comforting having him there in the middle of the night, easing my anxiety about Sully's crying jag.

He had been a good kid who had clearly grown into a good man.

He'd left early, waving off my offer of coffee. He'd been dressed all in black, with lots of metal lining his wrists, a skull hanging around his neck. The women who watched the reality show were going to love him. He was easy to look at, that was for sure. Especially without a shirt on. Not that any of them would see him without a shirt on. Right?

"I need your next clothing capsule video by Friday," Xander said. "And Chloe needs a consult on her subscription box series."

I nodded, forcing myself to focus on the content editor.

Xander Billings had hired me three years ago, and had been an easy boss, and helpful mentor. He was about ten years older than me, with impeccable style, and a brilliant British accent. His father was English, his mother Pakistani, and he'd been raised in London, but came to New York for a relationship.

The boyfriend hadn't worked out, but he'd carved himself a life in New York and had no plans to return to London.

"Anything else?" I asked.

"Yes. Are you going to explain to me why you're so distracted? Don't make me question letting you work at home. You know I'm a huge advocate for childcare."

I rolled my eyes. "I know you are. Don't worry. I'm going to be working primarily at night because I have a friend from my hometown staying with me for a few months. He works during the day but at night he'll be watching Sully so I can knock out my workload. He got here yesterday."

Xander's eyebrows rose. "*He*? Interesting."

"He's my little brother's best friend." I thought that would make Xander lose interest, and it somewhat did.

"Is he attractive?"

"Very. But he's covered in ink and looks like he belongs in a motorcycle club."

Xander shook his head. "Oh, that's not your type at all. Good. You already having an infant demanding your attention. You don't need a man doing the same. We have deadlines and the constant threat of competition chomping at our heels."

Then I would keep Operation Fix Up Savannah to myself.

And the fact that I had every intention of taking Sully to the park that afternoon. It was seventy degrees in October. I had to take advantage of the weather while I still could. It would basically be a crime not to.

"Think of my nanny as a positive, not a negative." That was how I was going to approach it. If Maddox could help me regain an ounce or two of my sanity, it was worth the occasional discomfort when my body felt the need to betray me and have a sexy response to him.

"I will assume, then, that I'll have that video in my inbox tomorrow."

Shit. "Of course. Absolutely. By the end of the day."

We ended our call and I swiveled my chair around, sighing. Fall in Barcelona. I needed to pull that video out of my butt in twenty-four hours. Time to pack up Sully and hit the stores for some affordable inspiration. The concept of the capsule wardrobe was key pieces that you packed for a vacation that could be readily mixed and matched. I gave all the links to online purchase sources, obviously, but most of the features had me wearing the combination of outfits, so I usually shopped at a handful of standard stores in a variety of price points.

The company comped me, so it was something I usually loved doing. Free clothes are never a bad thing.

But it was a different story shopping with a six-month-old.

As I worked on the holiday outfits article, I got a text from Leah.

Grant's cousin.

She followed that up with a picture of a good-looking guy standing in front of a sailboat. I zoomed in. Yep. Definitely attractive. He was wearing shorts, boat shoes, and a button up shirt in a pastel plaid. Caramel-colored hair, casually tousled. The smile of a man who has the world by the balls but isn't a prick about it.

Oooh, he's cute.

That is his sailboat, by the way. Too bad it's not summer.

I let my mind wander for a split second. Summers in the Hamptons. A house in Connecticut. Fabulous vacations, private schools, a wardrobe to die for. I wasn't seeking out a wealthy lifestyle, but I wouldn't say no to it either.

Sully, who was napping, coughed in his sleep. I let go of the fantasy and listened to hear if he was going to wake up or not. No further sounds emerged from the bedroom.

Did you mention me to him?

Not yet. Give me a current pic and I'll let Grant be the go-between. Unless you just want me to send him to your YouTube channel.

Ew, no! That's weird.

I did not want him seeing me posing in floppy hats for summer in Switzerland. Not until after he met me in person.

It's not weird, it's practical.

Practical is not cute. I'll send you something later. I have to finish this article right now. Work-life balance is a struggle.

Leah sent laughing emojis back.

Can I send him to your social media?

No! Just wait, I'll send you a pic.

I wanted it perfectly curated to the receiver.

It occurred to me that might actually be the worst possible thing to do, but it didn't stop me from devoting ten minutes to scouring my phone for an image of me in crop pants at the beach in August.

I sent it to Leah.

Why is this better than your Instagram?

I don't want him seeing random pics.

As I went back to my article, determined to focus and knock it out, she just sent me a "kk" text.

Sully started crying, effectively ending my worktime.

"I'm an idiot," I told my empty apartment. I'd wasted time searching for a photo when I should have been working. "I might even be hopeless," I said, even as I lifted my phone off my desk and stared at the image of the man Leah had sent.

What's his name?

I held my phone in my hand as I stood up to go get the baby.

Yates.

Is that his first name or last name?

First. Yates Caldwell.

I sent a wide-eyed emoji back and shoved my phone in my back pocket.

Sully had rolled onto his stomach and was lying there crying. He instantly stopped when he saw me. I smiled and reached for him.

Good on paper wasn't always good in real life. Like Sullivan's father. I needed to remember that.

"I'm just going to keep an open mind and live in the

moment," I told Sully in a singsong voice. "That's all I can do, right? No expectations. Just meeting new people."

He smiled, like he actually believed me.

I HADN'T THOUGHT WORKING with a camera crew all around me was going to bother me, but after a morning of introductions and being shown around the shop, I wasn't sure I was going to be as cool with it as I'd thought. It made for a crowded room and the producer would interrupt to interject questions to engage me and the customer to make it more interesting.

We weren't actually tattooing, just doing mock-ups to get the feel for it and I wasn't sure I loved any of this.

Eye on the prize.

That's what I had to remind myself.

Cameras were a byproduct.

I needed this gig for the money and the exposure.

And the access to Savannah.

The shop itself was pretty insane. I loved the vibe of being around all artists my own age and the décor was rock'n'roll. Exposed brick, black glass chandeliers, massive art pieces on the walls. The chairs were open-concept, which was different for me. I was used to working in a private room, but I thought I was actually going to appreciate the natural light.

They were only featuring five of us on the show. Three guys and two women. Travis was the owner of Rebel Ink and he was a tall, skinny guy with gauges in his ears, a nose piercing, and glasses. He was like the cartoon Waldo but with tats and piercings. Samuel was the youngest at twenty-one, Haitian, with an infectious laugh. I could easily imagine teen girls watching the show and falling hard for him with his easy charm. Stella was a blonde from Texas and didn't fit in with the stereotypical tattoo artist. She had very few tattoos herself and no piercings. She was wearing a hot pink shirt with ruffles. First impression, she was sweet, but I couldn't quite get a read on her. I clicked instantly with our fifth artist, Jana. She was petite, wore skinny jeans and Converse, and said it like it was. We all had different backgrounds, and different tattoo areas of specialty.

Having no experience with filming, I just kept my mouth shut and did as I was told. The producer was cool, and overall I felt like I could handle whatever he needed me to do to make the show interesting. The work itself didn't intimidate me. I'd been chosen because I did a ton of blackwork, meaning inking only in black. It required a lot of shading skill and I was proud of my work.

It was an intense morning, and when the producer told us at two we could leave for the day, I was cool with that.

"Hey, you want to grab something to eat or go to the park?" Jana asked me. "It's nice outside today and I want to get a little bit of a glimpse at Brooklyn."

I figured I still had a couple of hours before Savannah would expect me at the apartment. "Sure, sounds good."

She leaned closer to me and gave me a guilty look. "I would ask Travis and Samuel because they're cool, but then I'd have to ask Stella."

I raised my eyebrows. "What's wrong with that?"

"She's not my people." Jana gave me a shrug and a grin. "That makes me sound horrible."

Horrible was extreme, but it seemed like a quick judgment. "You just met her."

She looked around to make sure no one was listening. She gestured to the front door, so we waved to everyone in the room and left the shop. It was warm outside for October. I stretched and fell into step beside her as she started down the sidewalk.

"I was bullied in high school, like a lot of people. But an Asian lesbian is an easy target. Now I have a sixth sense for mean girls and she reeks of one. Maybe I'm wrong. We'll see. But I'm not going to waste energy trying to be friends with her when I don't think I'm wrong."

"I appreciate trusting your gut. Sometimes the gut steers you wrong though." I gave her a smile. "I could be a total dick for all you know. You might regret hanging out with me."

She waved her hand. "Nah. You're the kind of guy who looks tough but is a total softie. I bet you like puppies and babies."

I nodded. "Guilty. And I can't claim to know what it feels like to be you, so you're probably right. I didn't have a positive reaction to Stella, but I can't say it was negative either."

She pointed a finger at me. "But see? You had a neutral reaction, which for a cis man with a hot blonde is basically a negative response."

I wasn't even going to question how she had concluded I was a straight guy. She was also probably right on my reaction. "That is probably true. Though you're implying men can't think straight around hot blondes."

She gave me side-eye. "Well, can they?"

I pictured Savannah. "I prefer redheads."

That made her laugh. "It's not an insult. I go crazy for hot blondes too. It's biology. We're all susceptible to being stupid when we're attracted to someone."

"Do you have a girlfriend?" I asked as we crossed the street toward the park.

The whole vibe of the park was cool and interesting. The city had turned an old industrial area into greenspace and I found the mix of the natural with the manmade a fascinating juxtaposition. The trees were ablaze with fall colors.

"No, I just went through a shockingly easy breakup. We're still friends and everything is chill. How about you?"

I shook my head. "No."

"You hesitated," Jana said, giving me a mischievous smile. "So there is someone, just not an officially defined boyfriend/girlfriend situation."

"Are you sure you're a tattoo artist and not a sociologist or clairvoyant?" For barely being five feet tall, Jana was a little terrifying.

"I can just sense it. Do tell, Maddox. All your secrets are safe with me."

"I don't have secrets. I just want one woman in particular, that's all." I stopped walking abruptly.

A woman who was in front of me. Right now.

My heart and my cock both reacted the way they normally did around Savannah, tightening.

What were the odds? We were only a few blocks from her apartment but the timing was perfect.

She was pushing a stroller down the path in our direction. I'd recognize her anywhere. She had a colorful scarf wrapped around her neck, her hair piled on her head. She saw me a second after I saw her.

"Maddox!" she said, her mouth splitting into a smile as we met each other on the path.

"Hi," I said, running my hand over Sully's soft hair. "Hey, buddy."

The baby made a sound and lifted his arms, the universal gesture to be picked up.

"Can I take him out?" I asked. "I know how hard it can be to get babies back in the stroller once they're sprung."

Savannah waved her hand. "No, it's fine." She smiled at Jana. "Hi, I'm Savannah."

"Sorry," I said as I unclicked Sully and picked him up. He instantly reached for my necklace and lifted it up. "Savannah, this is Jana, from Rebel Ink. Jana, this is Savannah. And this is Sullivan." I took my necklace out of his grip when he started to shove it in his mouth and tossed it around so the skull was dangling on my back out of his reach.

"Nice to meet you."

"You, too." Jana was eyeing the situation with clear comprehension.

Savannah was a redhead.

Jana liked to assess things.

She was definitely onto me.

"How is the show going?" Savannah asked.

"So far, so good," Jana said. "We're done for the day. We were just going to grab something to eat if you want to join us."

"Oh, thanks for the invite, but I have a ton of work to do. Maddox, are you okay with watching Sully later? I have a piece I have to turn in by tomorrow."

"That's fine. Just give me a time you want me there."

"Perfect, thanks. I'm going to head home now. This working-mom thing is no joke."

I lifted Sully up in the air so he squealed in delight, then pulled him down and kissed his chubby cheek. "See you later, little man." I returned him to the stroller and clicked the strap to lock him in.

Savannah turned the stroller and waved goodbye.

I just watched her walk, appreciating her ass in her tight jeans.

"Bench. Now," Jana said, pointing to a free park bench in the opposite direction.

She sounded so fierce I was amused. "What? Why?"

"Because I'm going to explode if I can't talk in the next thirty seconds and I need her out of earshot."

Jana did look like she was going to burst. She was bouncing on the balls of her feet and twisting her long hair into a cone.

We went and sat down. "It's not what you think," I said.

"I knew you liked babies," she said. "God, I'm good." She eyed Savannah, now just a speck exiting the park. "But I have to say, I didn't actually think you *had* a baby. Or a baby mama that you're clearly still one hundred percent in love with. So what wrecked the relationship?"

"Slow your roll," I said dryly. "Sully is not my son."

Her eyes widened. "Oooh, so she cheated and got knocked up? Damn."

That was a horrible fucking thought. "No. We were never together. We're friends. Her brother is my best friend. We grew up together. While I'm doing the show, I'm staying with her. In exchange for a place to live, I watch the baby when she needs me to."

"Is the baby's father around?"

"No."

Jana nodded. "I figured as much. No man wants a muscular tattooed old friend as a nanny, living with his girlfriend."

"It's not like that. Savannah thinks of me as a little brother." Unfortunately. For now.

"But you do want to be with her, right?"

I wasn't sure why I was being honest with Jana when I'd just met her, but on the other hand, it seemed like she already had an accurate read on the situation, so why pretend I wasn't head over ass for Savannah? "Yes." I leaned back against the bench and put my ankle over the opposite knee, studying my work boots.

"Then make a play for her."

I had every intention of doing that, but didn't feel like I needed to spell out my actions to Jana. "It's complicated."

"Do you think she thinks you're hot?" Jana pulled both of her knees up to her chest and rested her feet on the edge of the bench. "I would assume most women would think you're hot. You have the right package."

I gave a scoff. "Thanks. I think. And yes, given things she's said, she thinks I've grown up just fine. But she doesn't want to go there. She's got her friends setting her up on dates."

"And you're just going to sit and watch her wind up with someone else?"

"I'm waiting for the right moment." The sun felt fantastic on my face and I tipped my head back.

"You just want to wait around and hope something happens?"

"I didn't say that. I just need to lay the groundwork."

I could feel Jana staring at me. "What?" I asked.

She shook her head. "Nothing. So let's lay the groundwork."

I eyed her. "I don't think you can help me with that, but thanks."

"I can plot with the best of them. What are her favorite activities, foods, movies?"

"She loves romantic comedies," I said, without hesitation. "And fashion."

"Oh, Maddox, this is gold. We can set up every rom-com moment. She'll be eating out of your hand in a month." Jana held her hand up to give me a high five.

"We're high-fiving?" But I did it, because I loved her enthusiasm. My only friend in New York was Savannah. It would be nice to have an ally if Jana was serious about all of this. "And what rom-com moments?"

"You need to do research online. But basically, we need you to save her from her boss, get her a promotion, be her confidant, accidentally slow dance with her, or pretend to be her boyfriend at a wedding. Maybe eat a pizza with her on a fire escape and almost kiss about ten times."

"All of those?" That seemed daunting and absolutely fucking ridiculous.

"That's just a jumping-off point. It doesn't have to be those specifically." Jana waved her hand. "We'll work out the details. But every day when you're with her you need to think WWRR."

I eyed her. "What the hell does that stand for?"

"What Would Ryan Reynolds Do."

That made me roll my eyes. "You forgot the D. You said WWRR. What Would Ryan Reynolds."

She thought a second. "Shit. You're right." She grinned. "Trust me to forget the D."

I laughed. "It doesn't matter. I never would have figured that out anyway."

"It's a great benchmark. Stop and consider what Ryan Reynolds or really any Ryan would do. Gosling works too."

Yeah, fuck that. "With all due respect to the Ryans, I'm not going to live my life copying some other dude's moves. I've got my own moves."

Jana looked dubious. "Don't be cocky. You don't need to reinvent the wheel, son."

I laughed. "So you're an expert? I'm sorry if I misunderstood that," I said dryly.

"Totally an expert. I date women, don't I? Oh, and you must discuss her dates with her."

"I don't want to do that." Nope. Not at all.

Jana smacked my leg. "You have to be her confidant! It's a requirement."

I laughed. "You're taking this very seriously."

"I love a project. Besides, I don't like being alone and I don't know anyone here, so I've decided you're going to be my best friend."

"To what do I owe that honor?"

"I can tell you have sisters. Right?"

I nodded. "Three."

"And they're all younger, right?"

I eyed her. "Yes. You're a little freaky sometimes, you know that?"

"I've been called worse things." She stood up. "Are you hungry? Let's eat and plot your strategy. We need to put some things into motion."

I'm not one for having a total stranger tell me what to do, but Jana amused the hell out of me.

Besides, she was right.

I wanted Savannah.

I'd do whatever it took to make her mine.

Chapter 5

"You look great," Maddox said as I came out of my bedroom.

He was standing eating a sandwich over the kitchen counter, Sully on his hip. After working all day, he'd gotten back to the apartment and changed into flannel pajama pants. He looked like a pro eating and juggling a baby.

Having him around for the last two weeks had made my life a hundred times easier, including tonight when I had taken a stupid amount of time to get ready for my date with Yates Caldwell.

I stood in the hallway and smoothed the front of my black dress. "Are you sure? I'm worried maybe this isn't the right outfit. I feel like I'm giving off a little bit of a corporate vibe."

His eyebrows went up as he chewed. "Have you looked in the mirror? You look hot." He set down his sandwich and gestured to my chest. "That is not what I imagine when I think office environment. But if that's the case, sign me up. I'll work for the man with that kind of view."

I glanced down at my cleavage. It did look a little different in this dress than it did pre-baby. My tits were spilling up and over. "Should I change?"

"Why?"

Because I was panicking. "I don't know. Because I haven't been on a date in over a year."

"You don't need to change. You look amazing." Maddox

bounced Sully up and down. "Right, buddy? Mommy looks amazing."

Sully was looking at me like he knew I had a plan to go out and prioritize a man over him. His nose was wrinkling and his lip was starting to tremble. "Oh, God, he knows I'm going out. He looks like he's about to start wailing." I put my hand on my stomach, the pit already there growing. "I feel guilty."

"Don't feel guilty. You're entitled to a life," Maddox said. "We'll be fine. We'll have guy time. Now leave before he loses it entirely. Seriously, run."

He was right. Sully was winding up to let out a serious cry, his arms stretching forward for me. "Oh, ugh!" I ran up to Sully and kissed him. "Bye, baby, I love you."

"Have fun," Maddox said.

Sully launched himself at me, like a skydiver jumping out of the plane. Full trust, arms spread like a flying squirrel. Fortunately, Maddox had a good grip on him and he didn't fall, though Sully did manage to grab the strap of my dress.

I wrested it out of his hand, but not before my tit well and truly popped out. It just sprang forth like it couldn't wait to get out of the tight dress and be useful. I stumbled back, tucking it away, flustered as hell. Mostly because my child was now screaming for me and I felt like a jerk mom. But also, because it seemed on the daily my relationship with Maddox became more and more… intimate. We lived together well, with zero conflicts. We had a routine, a rhythm, a friendship that was easy and surprising.

Yet, he didn't seem to want anything beyond that. Once or twice, I'd thought he was holding back, but at moments like this, he seemed completely neutral about me. He didn't react to my nip slip at all. He said things like "You look amazing," with sincerity but no more sexual interest than say, Isla.

Which was great. That was the way things were supposed to be. It was exactly what I had asked him for—a friendship with no flirtation. He was a platonic friend and my nanny and I was going out with Yates Caldwell, who ticked all of my boxes.

It didn't matter that on a regular basis I looked at Maddox

and wanted him to take me against a wall and make me feel like a woman again.

Not going to happen. It would be messy and complicated and he didn't appear to want me anyway.

"He's going to think you're amazing," Maddox said. "Trust me."

His words shattered my thoughts about climbing onto his cock.

I grabbed my purse and ran in heels to the door. "Bye, thanks, Mad!"

YATES CALDWELL WAS as good-looking as his photo, that was true.

But he was no Prince Charming. He was literally the opposite of Prince Charming. He was Sir Dickhead, overlord of the land of pompous pricks.

And for me to say that? He was not nice. Very, very bad.

I sat across from him at a bar in the Financial District after he had refused to come to Brooklyn because he was "really fucking committed with some things at work" and needed to stay close to his office. Even though, you know, I had a baby. In Brooklyn. But I was willing to be optimistic and chalk it up to tone is off in text messages sometimes.

That was just the beginning. A teeny tiny red flag.

Once there, I ordered some calamari and a soda, but he had waved off the food menu and was on his second dirty martini. He didn't really attempt to make conversation. He just glanced around the restaurant and made rude observations about the other patrons, and labeled the service slow. After the waitress brought my calamari and retreated, he watched her walking.

"God, she could use a nose job," he said. "I feel compelled to tip her well so she can save up for plastic surgery."

I blinked, shocked speechless. "I… I don't imagine she needs your opinion," I finally managed. "Especially not an unkind one."

He looked at me like he was surprised. "I wasn't going to say that to her, but come on, it's not like she doesn't know she's ugly as shit."

I bit a piece of calamari, hard, wondering if I could get the check and get out, now, while I still had some faith in humanity. Yet at the same time I hesitated to call the waitress over in case she had heard anything Yates had said.

But wait. That wasn't all that sucked about him.

Yates looked at his watch. For the third time.

"Do you have somewhere to be?" I asked, feeling hopeful. Maybe he had an urgent meeting he needed to get to or a date with the devil to give him yet another piece of his mostly empty soul.

He shook his head. "I'm just checking my heart rate to see if you turn me on."

It took me a full thirty seconds to process what he had just said. "What?" I asked, caught completely off guard. Was he serious?

"Yeah. If I'm into you, my heart rate will increase."

Um…

"So you don't know if you're turned on by someone? It's a mystery to you?" That was just about the dumbest thing I'd ever heard. Who didn't know if they had the tingle with someone? No one is bewildered by their reactions to people. We know what they mean. We know the difference between attraction and anger and apathy. My blood pressure and heart rate were through the roof, and I knew one hundred percent it was because he was an appalling human being. It's not like I was mistaking that for wanting some sexy times. It wasn't hard to interpret what I was feeling.

"To be honest, I'm on the fence about you," he said. "I don't usually like gingers. I'm trying to gauge if that's affecting my ability to picture myself inside you."

Inside you? Had he really just said that?

"I'll be right back," I said, shoving my chair back and standing up. I grabbed my purse. I was tempted to just exit the bar and never return, but I wasn't convinced he would pay for my food. I headed toward the restroom to gather myself together, seeking out my waitress on the way.

I found the waitress near the bar in the back and I handed her my credit card. "Can you charge me for just the calamari?" I asked.

She nodded. "Getting out?" she asked sympathetically. "I got the feeling it was a first date, and trust me, in this neighborhood I see a lot of the self-important type. That guy reeks of it."

"Normally, I'm all for sticking it out, but this was too much." The worst being his comments about this very waitress, who was smiling and pleasant and had a perfectly lovely face. Ugh. Yates Caldwell needed to choke on his lemon slice.

As the waitress went to run my card, I dipped into the ladies' room and pulled out my phone. The girls and I had a group text. I wrote NEXT and hit send.

My phone buzzed. I had a text from Yates.

Dude, not feeling the redhead. She's kind of a bitch.

The blood drained out of my face. He had sent me a text criticizing me to me. To. Me. Was that intentional or had he actually meant to send it to a friend? Not that it mattered, honestly.

And wait a minute. Me, a bitch? I've been called any number of things—naïve, gullible, a Pollyanna—but never a bitch. Apparently, even mildly calling him out for being a shallow prick about the waitress made me a bitch.

I freshened my lipstick and smoothed my hair in the mirror before rolling my shoulders and pushing the door open. I got my credit card back from the waitress, and signed the slip leaning on the bar. Then I just went back to the table, purse in one hand, my phone in the other, feeling outraged on behalf of all women who had to put up with arrogant, rude men.

"You texted me that you think I'm a bitch," I said. "So this bitch is going back to Brooklyn. If you're not sure how to feel about that, check your watch."

With that, I left. He didn't say a word.

It was his best move of the night.

. . .

THE DOOR OPENED and I looked up, surprised. Savannah had only been gone ninety minutes. An hour of that had to have been travel time.

"Hey," I said, on the floor on my stomach playing with Sully. I was building blocks for him and he was alternating knocking them down and chewing on them. "That was quick."

Savannah blew her hair out of her eyes, closed the door, and flung her purse on the end table. "That was a total waste of time. Yates was gross. A total jerk who told me he was going to tip the waitress really well since she badly needed a nose job."

"What?" I rolled over and sat up. "Who the hell says something like that? Out loud?"

"He also sent me this text when I went to the restroom." Savannah handed me her phone.

I read the text. "Is he talking about you?" I asked, outraged. "What the actual fuck?" Then I realized what I had said and covered Sully's ears. "You didn't hear that."

She was so outraged by her date, she didn't even reprimand me for swearing in front of the baby. "Yes, I'm sure he is talking about me. I guess it was an accident, but that was enough for me. I left. Maybe it wasn't an accident. I don't know."

"You are the last person in the world I would call *that*," I said, remembering to avoid swearing. "I'm glad you left, though I'm tempted to go punch him in the face."

"What a waste of a tight dress," Savannah said, holding on to the arm of the couch and ripping her heels off. She tossed them in the direction of the rug by the door.

It would have been a total waste of an outfit, except I definitely appreciated it. Her legs were a mile long, showing lots of creamy fair skin, and she had on full makeup. "It is a cute outfit," I told her. Even now, my eyes were going straight to her chest. I couldn't help it. There was too much skin not to look.

Savannah gave a little laugh. "Cute?"

"I'm trying to be supportive but not hit on you," I said. "And G-rated for the kid's ears."

She gave me a funny look but didn't comment. "I'm starving. I had one stupid piece of calamari."

"Let me fix you something to eat," I said, peeling myself off the floor with an eye on Sully to make sure he hadn't somehow miraculously in the last thirty seconds shoved something in his mouth he shouldn't. Babies are quick.

Savannah eyed me. "That's a sweet thought, but you don't cook."

I'd been living with her for almost two weeks, and she was right. She'd yet to see me cook. I had a protein shake in the morning, ate on set at the shop during the day, then I'd be back to her apartment to find she'd already made dinner for the two of us. "How do you know I don't cook?" I asked. "I have hidden talents you know nothing about."

She shrugged out of her long coat and hung it on the hooks by the door. "Oh, really? You're a master chef? Okay, then I'm sorry."

I strolled past her toward the kitchen and gave her a slow smile. "No need to apologize. I do have many hidden talents."

She heard the tone in my voice. For a second I thought she was going to reprimand me for hinting at something dirty but she didn't. So I said, "But truthfully, cooking isn't one of those talents, hidden or otherwise."

Her jaw dropped and she smacked my arm. "Maddox! You con. What on earth were you planning to make for me, then?"

"You have a cauliflower pizza in the freezer. I can turn on the oven, take it out of the box, put it on a tray, and put it in the oven. I can even take it out of the oven and use the pizza slicer to cut it in absolute perfect slices for you."

She shook her head and laughed. "What skill you have. It sounds perfect." She flopped on the couch. "Rage doesn't come easily to me. I'm exhausted from being angry with Yates."

"Whose date pick was this?" I asked, as I went into the kitchen. "I can't remember what you said."

I'd been following Jana's advice and being the friend who just listened as Savannah texted and DM'd with all these guys her friends were setting her up with. This tool was the first. I was pissed she'd been insulted by him, but I was selfishly glad it had gone down the way it had. It would suck if she'd come home dreamy and excited.

"This was Leah's pick. It was her boyfriend's cousin. I don't understand. Grant is a nice guy, but his cousin was a nightmare."

"Isn't he rich?" I asked as I pulled the box out of the freezer. "He could be that guy who just says whatever the hell he wants and gets away with it because he has money."

"Clearly. I mean, he didn't even seem to think it was a big deal. He acted like I was insane when I basically said it wasn't nice to insult the waitress's looks."

I turned on the oven and returned to the living room. I scooped up Sully and sat down next to her. I plopped the little guy between us. "At least he showed his ass up front. You didn't really waste much time."

"That's true." She sighed. "Dating is hard." Then she laughed. "The really stupid part? He kept checking his Apple watch to see what his heartrate was. When I asked him why, he said he was trying to see if he was attracted to me or not. That if he was, he would have an elevated heart rate."

I stared at her, uncomprehending. "What? That makes no sense. Wouldn't he just *know* if he's attracted to you or not?" The way I did. The way I looked at her and felt my cock harden. The way I wanted to peel her out of that tight dress and kiss down her body until I was burying my tongue inside her, tasting her as she moaned for me.

That's what I knew.

"Apparently, I'm a woman who has a man on the fence."

That seriously irritated me. "No, you're not. That guy is just a tool. That's a power move. He was trying to rattle you, get you to work harder to impress him." Which really made me want to punch him. "I'm glad you got out of there."

Savannah looked startled. "Really? Do you think so?"

"Yes. No one doesn't know if they're hot for someone or not. Come on. That's effing stupid. He was just messing with you, playing hard to get to switch the balance of power. If I had to guess, his goal was sex on the first date."

"Ew. That's gross and manipulative."

"Very." My gut told me I was right. There wasn't much other explanation for it. The oven beeped and I stood up to put the pizza in. "It's a fifty-fifty shot that text wasn't an accident either. He sounds like a guy who wants to be in charge of everything, all the time."

"That makes me feel like I need a shower."

I put the pizza in to bake and returned to the couch. "Who's on deck for your next date?"

"Dakota's choice. He's a club DJ."

Cool enough job, but not enough power to be a total dick. That could be bad for me. "When is that?"

"This week. Then in a few weeks I have Grant and Leah's engagement party to go to." She put her feet on the coffee table. "God, I just realized Yates will be there. That was so dumb. I should have just met him there and then decided if I wanted to go out with him. Now I'm going to spend the whole time avoiding him."

Sully had started to cry and root around for Savannah to feed him, so she eased up her sweater and unhooked her bra. We'd had a couple of discussions about the etiquette of nursing. She'd been trying to hide herself, using a blanket or leaving the room. I had told her there was absolutely zero reason to do that in her own home. That I respected and understood she was doing the most natural thing on earth—feeding her child.

I meant that. One hundred percent.

That didn't mean that seeing her bare flesh didn't make my mouth dry. Because it did. But I was glad that after only a couple of weeks she felt comfortable enough around me to be at ease with it. Of course, on the flip side, it also meant she had me solidly in the friend zone.

Being Mr. Nice Fucking Guy was backfiring on me and I hated it. I was starting to think I would be better off getting her so hot and turned on, that she begged me to fuck her.

That sounded way more fun than listening to her talk about other guys.

But I was still enjoying being around Savannah, hanging out

with her, getting to know her better as an adult, so I needed to calm down and be a little patient. My cock didn't agree.

"It's going to be a big engagement party, right?" I asked. "There will be a few hundred people there. You can avoid the ass — I mean, *him*."

"I just am annoyed that I have to spend the whole time thinking about him instead of having fun and celebrating Leah and Grant's happiness."

Jana and I had already talked about the impending engagement party. She'd wanted me to make a play to go with Savannah as her plus-one but I'd said that wasn't going to fly since I hadn't met any of her friends yet and I was needed to stay at home with Sullivan. But now… maybe I had an in.

"Want me to go with you? Show this guy someone finds you totally hot. It will annoy him you have another date so soon."

Savannah eyed me. "God, that's actually really tempting."

"Then let's do it."

"Why would you want to go to a party with people you don't know?" she asked. "And have to pretend to think I'm hot."

"I know you, that's enough for me. You should be able to enjoy yourself without worrying about some guy with zero manners. And I don't have to pretend you're hot, because you are. Hot." I studied her, wanting to bury my hand in her hair and pull her to me. "I don't need a watch to tell me that you're gorgeous."

She bit her bottom lip, teeth sinking in that delightful flesh as she turned to me. "You don't have to say that. Or take me to the party."

"I don't say anything I don't mean. Just like I don't have to tell you you're gorgeous and I don't have to go to an engagement party. I *want* to do both."

She patted my knee in a way that was so friendly and nonsexual it was frustrating. "You're very sweet. It would be fun to show Yates I'm not sitting around at home in need of a date. I think he thought he was doing me some sort of favor. I'd need to find a sitter for Sully. I have used a woman a few times in the past that was good. One of my co-workers recommended her."

"Give her a call and see if she's free." I stood up to check on her pizza before I showed her how my thoughts were the exact opposite of sweet. "Want me to grab your phone?"

"Sure. It's in my purse."

I brought her the purse she'd tossed down by the front door and left it beside her. I went into the kitchen and pulled out the pizza. I was a guy who liked to eat healthy but cauliflower just can't be pizza. It's too far of a reach. "You know," I said to her from the kitchen. "If a crap vegetable like cauliflower can reinvent itself as pizza, anything is possible. It's the ultimate dreams-are-possible food. It's very inspirational, though gross."

She laughed. "I like cauliflower! In all its forms."

"It smells like socks when you cook it." I set the pizza on the top of the stove and didn't think it looked very appealing. It looked pale and limp. "But I guess everyone has different tastes." As I dug through the drawers to see if she had a pizza cutter, because it seemed like if anyone would have one, Savannah would, I heard her greeting someone on the phone.

It sounded like she had called the babysitter.

I had nothing to wear to an engagement party, but I could sort that out. I wanted to go with her. I wanted to meet Yates Caldwell and have a little talk with him about how to treat women. I wanted to help Savannah feel confident and sexy. I rooted around in the drawer, my own confidence growing. I refused to stay in the friend zone. Or if I was in the friend zone, it was going to be a friend who had all the benefits of being able to touch her body.

Victory. She did have a pizza cutter. I cut her a slice and put it on a plate with a paper napkin. I brought it out and set it on the coffee table. I sat back down on the couch and waited for her to end her call.

"Ida can watch Sully." She lifted him up and pulled her shirt down. She put him over her shoulder and gently burped him. "Are you sure you want to do this?"

"Sure, why not? It will be fun." I played it casual. Then I reached out. "Now give me the kid and eat your cardboard covered in cheese."

"Hater." She passed Sully to me. "Did you eat something besides that sandwich?"

"I have to admit, I had a burrito delivered. The sandwich wasn't enough. But eating a burrito was stupid, because I haven't been working out as much as I'd like because of the show. I think I need to get up earlier and go to the gym before going to the shop." I slapped my gut. I swear, it felt like it was softening. "I don't want to get doughy."

She rolled her eyes. "I don't think that is going to happen in a few weeks. You're a rock. A complete rock. Granite."

That didn't suck to hear. "I want it to stay that way."

"How is the show going?" she asked, lifting her plate up to her chest.

I settled Sully into my lap. He wiggled his legs. I had to admit, I was falling for the little guy. He was one of the best babies I'd ever been around. Chill. Master of the spit bubble. Squealer enthusiast. He was becoming my little buddy.

"You know, it's kind of entertaining. I thought I would hate the scene setups and all that, but it's not bad. I've managed to stay out of the drama too."

"What drama is there?"

"Jana and Stella hate each other. It's like some weird random hate the second they laid eyes on each other. And Stella is hooking up with Samuel, which is not going to end well. He's just this guy having fun, charming as hell, and he thinks she's on the same page as him. But I'm convinced Jana was right in that Stella is not necessarily upfront with people. I think Stella will turn out to be more than Samuel bargained for." I didn't want to leap to any conclusions and assume she had stalker-girl potential, but it wouldn't surprise me if it went there. "And I cannot believe all of that just came out of my mouth. I may be spending too much time with Jana, Jesus. I sounded like a teenage girl."

Savannah laughed. "That was a little gossipy. Hooking up at work is always a bad idea. Both Samuel and Stella need to be careful. You and Jana seem close, by the way." She bit her pizza kind of viciously.

It seemed like I heard some jealousy there. She didn't know Jana's sexual orientation because it hadn't been relevant to any conversation I'd been having about her. Mostly I'd been talking about tattooing, not anyone at the shop's personal life. This was the first time I'd really dwelled into who was doing what. Let Savannah think what she wanted. Maybe it would be a good thing if she thought I had another woman interested in me. "Yeah, she's cool. We get along really well."

"Hmm," she said, not looking at me. She swallowed. "You've been spending a lot of time together."

We had. Jana and I had gone out for drinks a couple of times when Savannah didn't need me to watch Sully. Jana's upbeat attitude made her easy to be around. Plus, she loved to plot ridiculous scenarios of how I was going to win over Savannah and live happily ever after. In that respect, she and Savannah were actually similar in personalities. It was no wonder I liked being around her. I dug that sweet, generous, optimism.

"Yep."

My generic answers were driving Savannah crazy, I could tell.

"Maddy!" she said, sounding exasperated.

She only used my old nickname when she was annoyed with me or being super sentimental. It was obvious why she was using it now. She was totally jealous. I had to hide my grin. "What?"

"Are you and Jana, you know? Is she going to be upset if you go to this party with me next Friday?"

"Why would she be upset?" I asked, messing with her.

She threw her crust down on her plate. "You're being obtuse on purpose."

I laughed. I couldn't keep up the pretense. "She's not going to be upset. We're not, *you know*, as you so clearly put it. We're friends. Like you and me." It was a purposeful poke.

Her mouth opened, like she was going to say something. Then she clamped her lips together quickly.

When she continued to stay silent, I said, "Do you want me to be with Jana?"

She crumpled her napkin and tossed it in the direction of her plate. It rolled off and ended up on the floor. She ignored it. "If you want to be with Jana, be with Jana, obviously. She seems sweet."

"Do you think she's my type?"

I thought she would actually deny that she knew what my type was, but she nodded. "Yes, I do. She seems sweet and funny, and from what you've told me, she dislikes dishonesty and games. So that would be your type."

"True. But unlike Yates, your date from hell, I know when I'm attracted to someone and I don't have those feelings for Jana. She doesn't have them for me either. We're platonic friends."

She looked like she didn't quite believe me.

"Oh, and she's gay."

Her jaw dropped and she smacked my thigh. "You're ridiculous. You could have just said that in the first place."

"This was way more fun," I assured her. "And why did it matter to you so much anyway? You were very curious, Savannah."

Her cheeks turned pink. It was hard to hide a blush when you were a redhead. "What do you mean?"

That was a clear avoidance tactic. "You just seemed very interested in whether or not I was dating Jana."

"I just want you to be happy here."

Savannah was a terrible liar. She couldn't make eye contact and she picked at imaginary lint on her dress.

I put my hand over top of hers and stroked her skin with my thumb. "I'm very happy here."

Her head snapped up and her gaze met mine.

I leaned forward, wondering how she would react if I kissed her. I didn't think she'd stop me.

Almost imperceptibly, she leaned toward me.

Then Sullivan took a face dive. I snagged him before he toppled off my lap onto the floor.

"Oh, geez," she said. "That was close."

Yeah. It was.

Chapter 6

"Come outside with me," Jana said, holding her vape up. "I hate standing out in that alley by myself. It's like a crime waiting to happen."

"I have a client in ten minutes," I told her. "So I've got about five minutes, that's it."

"Fine, I'll suck fast."

"Someone is very friendly with Maddox," Stella commented as she walked past, wearing red high heels and shorts. For some reason, the fact that she wore heels to tattoo really pissed Jana off. "You two are *always* together. But you should hold out for better than giving out back-alley action, Jana."

"Don't be nasty," Jana said, shoving open the back door of the shop. "You know I don't suck dick."

"You're very crass," Stella said, sneering back at Jana.

Jana flipped her off.

The cameraman came with us, which didn't surprise me. The producer loved the tension between Jana and Stella. "Why is she such a bitch?" Jana seethed, putting her vape to her mouth and drawing in. "Someone is very friendly with Maddox," she mocked, using a terrible impression of Stella's Southern accent.

"Why do you let her get to you?" I asked, not out of judgment, but trying to understand.

"Because my whole life girls like her have been trash-talking me, and I'm sick of it. She has exactly zero reason to be a bitch, yet it's like she spends her days looking for ways to make other people feel bad about themselves."

"Maybe she has a past we don't know anything about. Maybe she's insecure." I didn't actually believe that, but I was trying to give the girl the benefit of the doubt. We'd only known her for a couple of weeks, and for all I knew, she'd been told by producers this was her role.

Jana snorted. "And maybe I'm in contention to play pro basketball."

"Let's assume, then, she is just a bitch who likes to make people miserable. You have to find a way to tolerate her. Otherwise, you'll lose your job and she'll win. Because filming or not, you can't be acting crazy in front of clients. People like that somehow always find a way to come out on top. I wouldn't count on it going in my favor if I were you."

She sucked on her vape, a plume of smoke rising in front of her face. "You're very pragmatic. I'm not sure if I love that about you or hate that."

I frowned. "I'm not sure I would call myself pragmatic." That sounded fucking boring.

"It's true. You're like a 'this is the way it is, so deal' kind of guy."

I leaned against the brick wall and stuck my foot against it. "I was raised by a teen single mom. That was the story of my childhood—deal."

"How old was your mom when she had you?"

"Fifteen." I was well aware the cameraman was filming, but I was proud of my mother. She'd worked her ass off.

Her eyes widened. "Oh, damn. That's young."

"Yep. She worked hard to provide for me, but we were broke, and she was gone a lot. So yeah, maybe I am pragmatic. But why does that sound like such an insult?" Women weren't going to be all hot for the guy who was pragmatic.

"It's not an insult. But right now, I just wanted to vent and rant and you wanted to problem solve. You're not a dude who sees the value in a grand gesture." She pointed her finger at me. "WWRRD, remember?"

I rolled my eyes. I was annoyed. I'm sure Ryan Reynolds was a great guy, but he played roles in movies. You know. Not real. They were lines in a script.

"What does that mean?" the cameraman asked. "Can you elaborate?"

"It means nothing," I said, opening the back door. "And no. I can't elaborate. I'm going back to work. I have a client."

I was doing a mountain scene landscape back piece and I was excited to get started on it. I held my hand out to the guy waiting for me and introduced myself. I welcomed the distraction from the conversation that had seemed to irrationally pissed me off.

Being a tattoo artist gave me a clear medium for my art and it had been a natural progression for me from comic book art I'd dabbled in during middle school and high school. It also had one big advantage over comics—I got to meet interesting people. Some people didn't want to talk, they were concentrating on dealing with the pain. But others wanted to talk through it and I was always up for that.

Even in a town that wasn't huge, I'd met people from all walks of life, with cool stories to tell. The meaning behind a person's ink always fascinated me. Some humbled me. Others had touched me in ways I couldn't have predicted, like a mother who wanted her child's footprint tatted on her own foot after the baby had passed away.

In that case in particular, I had been hugely honored that she had trusted an artist as young as me to do something so important, but she'd loved my portfolio. I had left after that appointment and driven straight to my parents' house to hug the snot out of all my siblings.

Nope, I didn't think of myself as a pragmatic guy. I actually thought I was kind of fucking sentimental.

But apparently unless you had a so-called grand gesture none of that shit mattered.

I wasn't sold on hanging back and being Savannah's nanny and honorary little brother and waiting for something to change.

If you want your situation to change, you do something about it.

I lifted the tattoo machine and asked the guy sitting on a chair with his back to me, "You ready for this?"

"Let's fucking do it," he said.

"Words to live by, man."

I'D GONE for a more casual look with Dakota's date choice for me. I was wearing wide-leg jeans, boots with a heel, and a tight off-the-shoulder sweater in a rust color that I hoped complemented my hair. I was wearing a jeweled headband to elevate the outfit slightly since this was a late-night date. To me, meeting a stranger for the first time at a club at eleven o'clock at night seemed a little odd, but Jackson Martin was a DJ. A *celebrity* DJ, whose day usually started at noon and ended at 4 a.m., so I had agreed to be flexible on when to meet up.

Yet at the same time, all I could think as I checked my lipstick in the mirror by the front door of my apartment was that I'd give anything to be sitting on the couch with Maddox and Sully right now. Maddox was lying down and Sully sitting on his chest.

"Hey, get your finger out of my nose," Maddox said, pulling Sully's hand back and giving his arms a little up and down motion. "That's nasty," he said in a teasing voice. "Yuck, yuck, yuckity yuck."

Which each yuck, he punctuated it by bouncing Sully up and down so that by the end, my son was laughing, that hearty belly baby laugh that warms your heart to the core.

It was stinking adorable. Just absolutely everything.

I was leaving that sound because I was determined that I was going to find my Prince Charming so that I could have a healthy, happy relationship with a man, and eventually, some day have more children. But suddenly my whole reason for doing all of these dates seemed suspect. Was I being totally selfish? Was it wrong to want to have a relationship right now?

I wished more than anything as I grabbed my purse that I

could do the casual sex thing. If I could just have the physical release and the satisfaction of being touched intimately by another person and not worry about it being anything more than that, I would be set. I'd be one happy mom and woman.

But I wouldn't even know where to start to just have a hookup.

As it turned out Jackson Martin did, unfortunately.

After I waved goodbye to Maddox and Sully and took a car service twenty blocks to where I was meeting Jackson, I went in to a super cool, super trendy bar. The vibe and the fashion excited me, I had to admit. This was where everyone came to have an Instagram moment. The bar even had the selfie wall, where you stood in front of it and the mural art painted on the wall gave you angel wings in your picture.

I spotted Jackson in the DJ booth, so I sat down at the bar, checking out the scene. I couldn't order alcohol, so once I asked for a water, the bartender's smile fell off and I got the "don't waste my time" expression. He filled a glass and slapped it in front of me, water sloshing over the rim.

My date had told me he wasn't working, so I wasn't sure what he was doing in the booth talking to the DJ, but it was clearly him. He was tall, thin, and had red hair, and it had been easy to find pictures on him online. It would be impossible to mistake him based on the hair alone. If this guy told me he wasn't attracted to gingers, I was going to lose all faith in dating altogether.

Five minutes ticked by before he finally made his way to the bar. He spotted me and gave me a wave. But instead of directly coming over to me, he actually stopped at the end of the bar and chatted up two blondes in their early twenties. Really? I was starting to get annoyed.

Then he moved toward me, finally, and gave me a big smile. "Hey! Sorry about that, business, you know, you have to make sure everyone is having a good time. It's hell to stay relevant these days."

I did understand that. Xander worried about that very issue constantly. "Oh, I get it. There is always someone behind us ready to be the next big whatever." I stuck my hand out. "I'm Savannah, it's nice to meet you."

"Jackson. Thanks for meeting up with me."

His smile was pleasant. I liked his height. I felt no particular attraction though.

"You're not getting a drink?" he asked, gesturing to my water.

"No, not tonight." I didn't want to get into the why with him. For some reason I couldn't pinpoint, I didn't want to talk about my son with him. "So, is this where you usually work?" I wasn't sure what to call DJing. Where you drop records? Where you spin the hits? Everything I considered saying sounded ridiculous in my head.

I had the sudden reminder that I had never been a club kid and so now, years later, this really wasn't my scene. It had never been my scene, so now it felt especially awkward. I was dressed completely wrong, which I had known I would be. I just hadn't wanted to waste another sexy dress on a first date. It felt like a man had to earn the tight dress. In a way, not being on display in a short dress, so similar to all these girls around me, made me feel more confident.

This was who I was.

Jackson gave me a low smile. "Do we really need to do that whole small talk bullshit thing? Where we pretend to get to know each other?"

I blinked. Didn't we? "I thought that was the whole point, to get to know each other."

"I don't need to know your middle name to peel you out of that sweater."

Um…

"That's your plan?" I asked. "To have sex tonight?"

He frowned. "Yeah, of course. Isn't that your plan?"

I sipped my water and fished an ice cube out with my tongue. I crunched it hard with my teeth, disappointed. "No, it wasn't. I thought this was a date, not a random hookup."

To his credit, he looked surprised. "Oh, shit, I'm sorry. I guess that was a total miscommunication. Dakota told me you're a new mom and that you needed to feel like a woman, get some D in the V and nothing else." He put his hand on his chest "That I can do. I can give you as much dick as you want. I can't date you, though.

I can't even keep a fucking succulent alive, I can't date a woman with a baby."

Really, Dakota? I was going to kill her. That's how she presented this whole thing to Jackson? I actually felt bad for him now. Here he thought he was going to get laid and I had just disabused him of that notion. "Oh my God, yes, this is a huge misunderstanding and I kind of want to kick Dakota's butt right now. I'm sorry, she should have *never* made it sound like that. While I appreciate your very generous offer of unlimited dick, I don't think I'm really wired like that."

Jackson made a face. "This is actually kind of funny, isn't it? I can't believe I said I can give you all the dick you want, I'm sorry. That was a douchebag thing to say."

"Under the right circumstances, it would actually be sexy," I assured him. "If everyone is on the same page, I say lean in to that. It's a good dirty talk maneuver."

He laughed. "You're being cool about this whole thing. I hope you're not offended that I said I can't date a single mom."

I waved his comment off. "Oh, please, no. I think it's awesome that you understand that about yourself and are being honest. I totally grasp not everyone wants an insta-family. Hell, my son's father didn't even want him."

"Now that's shitty," he said. "Once it happens, you have to be all in, whether it was planned or not."

"Thank you," I said. "I think so too. You're also being very cool about this, too, by the way. I'm sorry I can't fuck you."

"It could be fun," he said, tilting his head, giving me a grin that made me think he knew he had exactly zero shot of it working. "I believe in oral sex for all parties involved."

As it should be. I thought Jackson was kind of funny. Under different circumstances, if I were different, maybe. But nope. The club was loud, and it made conversation challenging. Since we didn't need to talk to get to know each other and I was not going to have sex with Jackson, I figured there was no point in sticking around.

"I applaud equal opportunity oral. Seriously. Every man should be you. But I still need to say no." I stood up. "So, I'm going to just go ahead and head home now and we can laugh about this tomorrow. I don't want to waste any more of your time." Mostly mine. I didn't want to waste mine. "I'm sure some woman will be more than happy to let you into her vagina. The night is still young."

"That it is. Be safe going home."

I gave Jackson a wave and left the club. Outside, I gave a sigh. After ordering a car, I texted Dakota.

You told Jackson I want D in the V?!?!

Well, don't you?

Yes, but that's not ALL I want.

So you had fun?

That actually made me laugh. Typical Dakota.

No. I'll call you tomorrow.

Jackson hadn't been a prick like Yates, but all of this could have been avoided by Dakota paying just a slight bit more attention. I shook my head, both frustrated and amused.

Whatever. At least I was reasonably close to my apartment.

As I got in the car that pulled up for me, I tried to imagine having D in my V.

I sighed again.

Sex felt like ancient history.

My body was dusty and mummified. Just a milk production plant, otherwise neglected.

Now I had to go home and share space with a muscular man who hated shirts and not touch him.

So not fair.

I WAS WATCHING a comedy stand up show on my phone, lying on the couch, when I heard the door open. What the hell? It was yet another speed date. Savannah hadn't been gone more than forty-five minutes.

Sitting up, I said, "Hey, you okay?"

She had eased the door shut, leaned against it, then barely gave me a wave before going straight to the kitchen. She didn't answer my question, so I stood up and followed her. Sully had gone down before she'd left so I didn't want to be shouting across the apartment for fear he'd wake up.

Her head was in the freezer. She pulled it back out, a pint of ice cream in her hand. She looked frustrated. Yanking the lid off, she slid her tongue across the cold surface of the ice cream.

Seeing her immediate satisfaction at the taste, her pink tongue inspiring dirty thoughts, I felt my cock harden. I was a total asshole, but man, I had to admit I was happy that her date must have been a bust.

"Do you want a spoon?" I asked, opening the drawer and retrieving one. I handed it to her.

"Thank you." She jammed it into the ice cream and scooped up a massive amount of the ice cream. "This guy thought this was a casual hookup. He wanted to skip conversation and get straight to sex. He told me he could give me as much dick as I want, but nothing else."

"What the fuck?" And yet another motherfucker I wanted to punch. I also was relieved she hadn't taken him up on his offer. To think that right now she could be underneath another guy was not cool.

"To be fair," she said, mouth full of ice cream. "Dakota basically told him I'm horny and need to get some, so I don't think he was working off the right parameters."

"You're not horny?" I asked.

"Of course I'm horny!" she said, stabbing the container again with the spoon. "Are you insane? It's been over a year since I had sex."

I held my hands up. "Sorry. I was just clarifying the situation. So, just confirming, you are absolutely, definitely in need and want of sex?" I had just seen a door open and I was walking right fucking through it. I wanted her. She wanted sex. I didn't want her getting it from another guy. No more laying the groundwork. It was go time.

"Yes! I want sex. Who doesn't?" Her cheeks were flushed now, though I wasn't sure if it was embarrassment or anger. She pointed the spoon at me. "You don't help, you know, walking around without a shirt, *or worse*, nothing, all the time."

Now that was what I was talking about. I pushed her, just a little further. "Then why didn't you want to hook up with this guy?"

Savannah looked at me like I was a disgusting and idiotic creature. "I don't want to have sex with a stranger. I want to have sex with someone I know. That's the problem. I want safety and sexiness and laughter. I want toe-curling, tension-relieving, now-I-can-face-the-day sex."

Best words I'd ever heard. I reached out and took the spoon from her. I put it in my mouth and stole her bite. Then I tossed the spoon into the sink. I leaned in, crowding her. The only thing separating us was the pint she was now clinging to like it was a shield. Dropping my gaze to her lips, I put my hand on her hip, stroking lightly.

"I can give you that," I said. "I can relieve your tension. Help you face the day. And I can most definitely get your toes to curl."

Her mouth fell open and she quickly dropped her gaze, sneaking a peek at me under her lashes. Then she lowered her head and stuck her tongue in the ice cream again. That almost made me groan out loud. There was no way she didn't know damn sexy she was.

She raised her chin, the ice cream on her tongue. By the time she was pulling it back into her mouth, I was already bending to take her lips in a cold, and yet, hotter-than-fuck, kiss.

Chapter 7

I COULD HAVE SAID NO. I could have pulled away.

Maddox gave me plenty of time to do either of those.

But I didn't.

Not even close. I leaned in, ice cream still on my tongue, staring into his beautiful dark eyes. He smelled like he'd just showered, and as usual, he wasn't wearing a shirt. I wanted to touch his muscles, feel his warm skin against mine. I wanted to explore every inch of that very, very masculine body of his.

I'd been resisting temptation for weeks and now, I just couldn't manage one more weak-ass protest.

When he took my lips in a kiss, I closed my eyes and gave myself over to it. His mouth was firm, demanding, talented. I sighed, clutching the pint of ice cream with numb fingers. Maddox kissed like he'd been waiting for this moment—with focus and tenderness, with a teasing tongue and relentless touch.

His hands cupped my cheeks and I opened my eyes to see him pulling back slightly, to study me, fingertips brushing against my skin. "You're so beautiful," he said.

A shiver rolled through me. What the hell was I doing? "My hands are freezing," I murmured, in an attempt to disrupt the moment, recover myself.

Maddox took the pint out of my hands. He set it on the counter and rubbed my hands together gently. Oh, God. The way he was looking at me. I couldn't resist him. I had nothing in me to resist his intensity. He was taking me in like he wanted nothing more than me. He dipped his finger into the ice cream and painted my bottom lip with the sweetness.

Then he ate it off. First, he drew his tongue across my lip with an agonizing slowness that had my nipples tightening and my inner thighs warming.

I moaned softly as I grabbed on to his biceps for support. Those muscles. It was the first time I'd actually touched them, and they were everything I'd imagined and then some.

He dropped a soft kiss on the corner of my mouth, then moved his lips back and forth over mine, before sucking my bottom lip between his. Then he teased his tongue into my mouth and the sweetness of the ice cream combined with the heat of the kiss, of our arousal, and made for a delicious embrace.

I was leaning into him, without even realizing it, my body aching with want. I ran my hands eagerly down and up the length of his muscular arms. Maddox's hands dropped, found my ass, and pressed me harder against him. I felt the unmistakable ridge of his hard cock against my thigh. It should have been a wake-up call.

It had the opposite effect. I groaned. I wanted that. All of that. Inside me.

Somehow, and I honestly couldn't have explained how he managed to do it, my jeans were unbuttoned and Maddox had slipped his hand inside to cup me. I looked down in awe at the heavily tattooed hand and wrist descending into my pants, a finger stroking over my clit. Yet again I thought to wonder what the hell we were doing when he took my breath away easing into my panties and right into my wet, eager pussy.

He kissed the inside of my neck as he stroked me, his lips a hot path down my flesh, to the swell of my breast. He yanked the neckline of my sweater lower and kissed and stroked, stroked and kissed, until I realized that I was way too close to the edge. It had been too long. I was going to push him away, but then he found the most perfect angle inside me and I came without warning.

I was too stunned to make a sound. I just held on to him and panted as the quick release made me tremble.

Maddox eased his hand back and gave me a wicked smile. "That was part one."

"How many parts are there?" I breathed, stunned by what had just happened.

He didn't get a chance to answer. Sully let out a sudden and sharp cry that had me jumping with guilt and surprise.

"Oh, shit," I said, licking my bottom lip. "Was I loud? Did I wake him up?"

"You barely made a sound." Maddox gave me a soft kiss that was as confusing as it was arousing. "I'll get him."

Thank God. I wasn't sure I could look my baby in the eye right then since I'd just let his nanny in my pants.

After quickly zipping those pants, I slapped the lid back on the ice cream and shoved it in the freezer.

Maddox returned with a red-faced and sleepy Sully. "I'm not sure what's wrong with him," he said. "It was so sudden it might be teething. He was out like a light all night."

My brother's best friend turned nanny turned man who gave me an orgasm after thirty seconds looked casual AF. I was flustered and embarrassed. Now what? Maddox did not look concerned about the interruption or what had just happened, even though I could see in his loose pajama pants he still had a very hard cock. Just the sight of it made my mouth water. He saw me check him out. His eyebrows rose in acknowledgement that he'd seen me looking south.

"Another time," he said. "You'll get to have it, don't worry."

"Maddox!" I was actually shocked. He made me feel very much like a Victorian virgin. Well, except when he had me breaking on his finger. I just found it ironic that he could make me so flustered and off-kilter. Who the hell would have ever seen that coming? Not twenty-year-old me, that was for damn sure.

My nanny turned torturer let out a crack of laughter at my admonishment.

I ran my hand over Sully's head and wiped his fat tears off his cheeks. "Shh, it's okay, buddy. You're okay." I looked at Maddox over his head. "Maybe it's a good thing he woke up. What the hell just happened between us?"

"Is that a rhetorical question?"

"No! It's a serious question. We can't just be randomly making out and… doing things." Sully reached for me and I took him, bouncing him up and down automatically.

"We can't?" He just looked amused. "It seems like we just did."

"Stop being so casual." My cheeks felt hot and I wasn't even sure why. "We're supposed to be friends."

"We are friends, Savannah." Maddox brushed my hair back off my cheek, making me shiver. "But we're also hot for each other. Just admit it. The sky isn't going to fall if you do. They even have a phrase for it—friends with benefits."

I chewed my bottom lip, frustrated. "This is a bad idea."

"What is? Giving each other pleasure? That seems like a fantastic idea to me." He gave me a slow, crooked grin. "And you didn't deny you're hot for me."

I didn't. I couldn't. "You've been walking around shirtless on purpose, haven't you?"

"I don't like shirts," he said. "It's not my fault you enjoy the view."

I rolled my eyes. "I'm going to change Sully and see if I can get him back to sleep. This conversation isn't over."

"Good. I could have this *conversation* all night."

Oh, my. That was promising and terrifying all at once. Maddox looked like he had any number of things he wanted to say with his tongue all over my body. And Lord, did I want the man to talk.

I took Sully back into my bedroom and changed his diaper, distracted. So, I'd let my nanny get me off. That wasn't a huge deal, was it? There were worse things I could have done. Cheated on my taxes. Cursed a high school enemy with a voodoo doll. Reckless use of exclamation points in my work articles. Forgotten to call my mother on her birthday. Those were bad things. This was not.

It wasn't like I'd *asked* Maddox to do it either.

He seemed to be fully on board with some casual intimacy.

He was right—we were friends. If we kept it on the down low, did it really matter? Couldn't it be a mutually satisfying arrangement for the time he was staying with me? I thought about Steven's reaction. My brother would lose his shit. But he was in Stroudsburg and really, who I had sex with was my own business, not his. He didn't tell me a damn thing about his personal life.

That gave me exactly no reason to worry about Steven's feelings, right?

Sully had stopped crying almost the minute the soiled diaper was off, so I snapped him back into his pajamas and picked him up. I kissed his still-damp cheek. "This is our little secret, okay, sweetie? Don't tell Uncle Steven. Mommy needs a little boom-boom."

Even as I rocked him and spoke, he was already dropping back into sleep. Mercifully, within a couple of minutes he was out, body limp and heavy, lips parted as he breathed in and out. I put him back in his crib and watched him for a second to make sure he didn't wake back up. He stayed asleep, so I retreated to the bathroom, washed my hands, and contemplated brushing my teeth but then decided if I came out smelling minty fresh it would be super obvious.

I was insanely self-conscious. I adjusted the off-the-shoulder side of my sweater, trying to expose more skin without making it seem like I was. "You're ridiculous," I murmured to myself in the mirror, before sticking my tongue out at myself.

Going down the hall, I had the sudden urge to stop at the end of the wall and drape myself in the doorframe like a femme fatale. Except knowing me, I would trip and break my ankle. So instead I sort of fast-walked into the room and jumped onto the couch next to Maddox, tucking my feet under my legs. "Hi."

"Hi." He smiled at me. "Sully asleep?"

I nodded. "Wet diaper."

"Do you want more ice cream?" he asked, resting his hand very casually on my knee, like we sat like this all the time.

He was younger than me and yet I felt like a middle school girl all of a sudden. I was a mother, and I was unnerved by Maddox's hand of my knee, of all stupid things, very aware I was still wet from his touch. "No, I'm fine. I've already put my foot in my mouth, I don't need to put anything else in it."

The corner of his mouth turned up. "Nothing else? You don't want anything else to go into your mouth?"

I smacked his arm. "I realized exactly one second too late how that would sound."

He laughed. "When did you put your foot in your mouth?"

"I told you I want toe-curling sex, not with a stranger, or whatever I said. I didn't mean you had to step up to bat."

"What if I've been dying to play for *years*?" He stroked his thumb across my knee. "And you telling me that was basically like a coach yelling 'you're in!' to the benchwarmer."

I blinked at him. "You've been waiting to be told you can go in?"

Maddox nodded. "The first day I got here you put me in my place, so I've been waiting. I didn't want to fuck this up or make you uncomfortable, but the truth is, you're my teen fantasy and, Savannah..."

When he didn't continue, I asked, "Yes?" My heartrate had shot up and my inner thighs had suddenly gotten very, very wet.

"I want to strip you naked and worship every inch of your sexy body. I want to make you come so many times you don't even know your own name, then I'm going to start all over again and do the same thing a second time."

"Um..." I was speechless. And burning up from the inside out. My mouth was hot, my throat dry. "I..."

Maddox took my hand, lacing his fingers through mine. "But I want to be clear. I made you come because I wanted to pleasure you, not because I saw it as the price of admission to your body. You call the shots here."

With that, his words both startled me and reassured me. He was a man who had been raised to respect women, and I realized that initially he had flirted with me, but just that first day. As soon as I'd told him I wasn't interested, he had backed off and established himself as my babysitter and friend.

I was so going to have sex with him.

Untucking my feet, I shifted and climbed onto his lap.

He made a sound in the back of his throat that I didn't think I would ever forget. His nostrils flared as I sank my thighs down, knees on either side of him. He gripped my waist, me his shoulders, as I leaned in.

"If I'm calling the shots, I want you to do what you said. What was it?" I asked. "Strip me naked and worship every inch of my body?"

"Your *sexy* body," he said, voice low and rough. "That's what I said."

I gave him a smile. "Yeah. That. Do that."

SAVANNAH WAS ON MY LAP, her smooth fingers gliding over my shoulders, across my biceps. This was happening and I was one lucky motherfucker. I could feel the warm press of her pussy against my cock, even through her tight pants. What I really wanted to do was just yank her jeans off and fuck her hard, fast.

But that would mean the fun would be over way too fast. I wanted to draw this out. Make it last as long as I could handle without exploding. I ran a finger over the creamy skin exposed on her right shoulder. Her sweater had slipped and even that glimpse of her flesh turned me on. She had the ivory skin of a redhead, but whereas she covered the freckles on her face, her shoulder showed a dusting of them. I wanted to kiss each one.

So I did.

Her soft hair brushed against my cheek and she sighed, rocking herself just ever so slightly against me.

I lifted my head and said, "Kiss me, Savannah."

She tossed her hair back, then gave me a soft smile. I couldn't tell what she was thinking, but it was enough to me that she was here, on my lap. I expected a sweet kiss. It wasn't. The second she leaned in, she was hungry, questing, pressing her mouth eagerly against mine.

Damn. Sweet Savannah was Sexy Savannah.

She was pressing her tits against my bare chest, and sliding her tongue between my lips.

I gripped her hips, hard, kissing her back, fighting her for domination, wanting her so fucking bad. She was giving the sexiest little moans and I could feel the tightness of her nipples through her thin sweater. Her nails pressed into my arms.

We devoured each other, both not able to get enough, until I flipped her off of me and onto her back on the couch. I'd give anything to take her to a big bed, but I couldn't risk Sully waking up and cock blocking. We had to stay in the living room, and no getting her to screaming levels, unfortunately.

I popped the snap on her jeans for the second time in one night. "We have to be quiet," I told her. "No waking the baby."

She nodded. "Silent sex. I can do that. Whatever it takes to have you inside me."

Holy fuck. Nothing could be hotter than hearing her say that. "I need to go get a condom out of my bag. Don't move."

Having a teen mom had meant she'd beat into me the importance of protection. Most of the talks had gone along the lines of "I'm not watching your kid if you screw up" and "babies are expensive." I had believed her and as a result always had condoms in easy access.

I was back in a minute, condom on, pants off, and she was lying on her back, hair spread around her shoulders. For a second, I felt like I couldn't breathe, she was so damn gorgeous. And she was still fully dressed. I put my knees between her thighs, easing them apart, and looked down at her. Cupping her cheeks, I gave her a slow, deep kiss. Then I eased her sweater up and over her head before tossing it onto the floor.

"Can you…" She took a deep breath. "Maybe stay away from my chest? The nursing… it feels awkward."

I nodded. "Of course." The last thing I wanted was for her to feel self-conscious or to feel like a mom instead of a woman. I was well aware of what she had admitted—she hadn't had sex since before Sully was born.

It was probably best to just leave her bra on unless she indicated otherwise.

I kissed her, wanting to erase that nervous expression she was wearing.

I'd always wondered what it would be like to kiss Savannah. In my nerdy teen years, I had imagined she would be cool and sophisticated, a bit icy. But she was anything but. Savannah opened herself easily to me, and wrapped her arms around my back, nails scratching lightly across my skin. So lightly it gave me goose bumps.

It was a warm kiss, a sweet brushing of our mouths, an honest and vulnerable touch that heated higher with each touch, each stroke. My muscles tensed, my cock hardened, as she made those sounds of pleasure, little moans of eagerness. It was better than any fantasy I'd ever had.

When she started to shift her hips, questing, her nails no longer as light on my skin, I pulled back. There was only one lamp on in the living room and it was the perfect amount of illumination on her pale skin. "Savannah."

"Maddox." She stared up at me expectantly, trusting.

"You turn me on so fucking bad." Then I gripped both her panties and her jeans with my hands and dragged them down. I got them off one ankle and then the other.

I went back to her mouth, kissing her hard, crowding her body with mine. Running my hands over her shoulders, down her arms, I brushed over her fingers and then shifted to her hips. She had an hourglass shape. Big breasts, narrow waist, full hips. I'd spent enough time staring at her as a teenager to know it was her natural shape, but definitely more exaggerated now that she'd had a baby. Everything about it turned me on. She was soft, with silken skin, and curves that had a little give to them. Not skin and bones.

As I stroked her hips, her inner thighs, just getting the feel of her body, and her reactions to what areas, I kissed the trail behind my touch.

She tensed and tried to shift away when I touched her stomach, so I moved on. But otherwise she seemed relaxed and aroused. When I got to her inner thighs with my mouth, dropping a light kiss on one thigh, then the other, she gave a little sound of both pleasure and impatience.

Trying to turn so I landed on her pussy, Savannah reached down and buried her fingers in my hair. I had beard stubble and I lightly rubbed against the tender flesh, still not going where she so clearly wanted me to. Drawing out the tease, I skimmed right over her sex and lifted back up to give her another aggressive, hard kiss.

This time she wrapped her foot around my calf and drew her body closer to mine.

That's when I went back down and slipped my tongue over her clit and down inside her. She gave a hiss of ecstasy, clearly trying to stay quiet, but her nails dug deep into my skin. "Mad..." she whispered. "Oh, God."

Mad. She'd given up calling me Maddy.

It was a fucking satisfying realization. I dropped my tongue in and out of her, finding a rhythm. She was deliciously wet and trying to take more from me, lifting her hips.

"I need to come," she murmured.

I shook my head. "Not yet." Using the strength of my forearms I held her knees down, spreading her even wider. "I want to look at you."

She was bare, pink, swollen, and very, very wet. I stroked along her folds, breathing in her feminine scent. I wanted everything about this night to be burned in my memory forever. I tasted her clit, and I used my finger to ease inside her in search of the angle I'd found earlier, the moment that had caused her to shatter with almost no warning.

"I can't..." she said. "I need to move. It's too much. It's too intense, I can't."

Then she was exactly where I wanted her to be. Using both tongue and finger to drive her insane for another second, I pulled back entirely. She let out a cry of agony.

"What the hell are you doing?"

I looked up at her, wiping my bottom lip. "You told me it was too much. You said you needed to move."

Savannah's cheeks were bright red from arousal, her eyes

glassy. Her mouth dropped. "No, no, that's not what I want." She lifted her hips, bumping my arm with her thigh. "I just meant I wanted to move. Please. Please, don't stop."

Nothing had ever sounded hotter than that.

I buried my mouth into her pussy and took her with my tongue until she burst into an orgasm. She gave a momentary cry, before she slapped her hand over her mouth to stifle it. Her body jerked, and moisture met my touch. Her legs were shaking.

Everything about it was amazing.

When she finally stopped shuddering, I shifted her legs as far apart as I could on the couch.

She looked down at me. "You knew exactly what I meant, didn't you? You're a very bad man."

"That I am," I said, and I pushed inside her wet heat. "Fuck, Savannah…" I closed my eyes briefly, wanting to savor the moment. My cock was throbbing inside her and she had given a deep, low moan.

"Yes, Mad. Fuck me."

I wanted to do nothing more than that. "My pleasure." I moved inside her, thrusting hard, finding a fast, pounding rhythm.

Savannah had wrapped her ankles around my legs and dug her nails into my back. The harder she pressed into my flesh, the more it turned me on. She was enjoying me inside her. Her eyes were closed, lips parted, a little gasp of pleasure slipping out with each hard thrust.

She was tight and very wet. She was pure perfection, and when she swore under her breath and arched her back, I watched her orgasm with awe. Her cheeks and neck had flushed pink from arousal and her eyes were glassy. That gorgeous red hair was spread across the couch cushion and I brushed it off of her forehead, wanting to feel the silken strands.

I was torn between the agony of wanting to explode inside her and the raw determination to enjoy it as long as I could. I'd been waiting damn near ten years for this and I didn't want it to end. Ever.

Slowing my movements, I fell into taking her in a more tender, deeper penetration. I kissed her, briefly, wanting a total connection.

When I pulled back, I realized she was on the edge again. Reaching between us, I teased at her clit with my finger and she exploded quickly, giving out a sharp cry. She didn't even seem to realize she'd made a sound, and that made it even hotter.

Seeing how fully she was into the moment, how good she clearly felt, I couldn't stop my own explosion. I came with gritted teeth and her name on my lips in a low growl.

When I finally stopped moving, she was looking up at me in shock. She gave a little laugh. "What just happened?"

"Sexual perfection, that's what." I eased out of her and fell on my side next to her, sliding my hand over her hip.

She sighed in contentment. "I really needed that."

Me, too. "I'm always here to give you what you need."

I meant that.

She gave me an odd look though. "You're going to fall off the couch. I should get up."

"I'm fine." I was hanging halfway off, but I didn't care. Savannah was mostly naked and next to me. I had zero complaints.

"I should go to bed anyway." She struggled to sit up, pushing my hand off of her hip.

She was retreating. Her gaze was darting all around and she was grabbing at her clothes. The minute I'd stopped touching her, she'd seemed to panic.

It didn't thrill me, but I would let her go. I didn't want to make her uncomfortable and I didn't want her to have any regrets. I would prefer an invitation to her bed so that I could fall asleep with my body touching hers, but I knew she wasn't going to suggest that.

Sullivan might only be six months old, but he had a routine, and me in his mom's bed was not part of it. I sat up so she could stand, though I did indulge myself by sliding my hand across her bare ass. She jumped a little, clearly startled.

As she bent at the knees to scoop up her pants, she finally looked at me. "This isn't going to be weird, is it?"

"Not at all. I promise." I gave her a smile, resting my arms on my knees, ignoring the condom for now. "It's going to be nothing but satisfying."

She nodded, but she didn't say anything. "Okay. Well, thanks for, you know, everything."

I raised an eyebrow. "You're thanking me? Is that for giving you an orgasm? Because trust me, the pleasure was all mine." I stood up as she made a sound of exasperation and clutched her clothes to her chest.

"See? I'm making it weird. I don't know what else to say!"

I gave her a kiss. "How about good night. I'll see you in the morning. Sweet dreams."

"Good night. I'll see you in the morning. Sweet dreams," she parroted. Then she bit her bottom lip and eyed me with naked lust. "And it was three orgasms," she said. "I'm thanking you for three."

With that, she turned and went straight into her bedroom and closed the door.

Damn. I was definitely one lucky motherfucker.

Chapter 8

WAKING up alone after a night of amazing sex wasn't strange in and of itself. I'd had plenty of boyfriends and dates who rolled out at three in the morning on occasion for various reasons. What was weird about waking up alone was the man I'd shattered beneath was sleeping on my couch.

Friends with benefits. That's what we were. No big deal.

Except he slept on the couch in my apartment and he watched my child.

Yeah, that wasn't complicated at all.

Also, the whole point of having my friends choose dates for me was because I sucked at picking out men and I attached easily. Like, you boned me, and I was half in love. We all knew that.

So, what made me think it made one single ounce of sense to have sex with Maddox?

I sent a group text, still in bed, mildly freaking out. Or a lot freaking out.

HELP.

That should get a response quickly. Felicia answered right away.

What's up?

Can anyone meet for coffee in like an hour, two tops? I NEED to talk.

Isla and Felicia agreed to meet me. Leah and Dakota were silent and I realized they were probably both still sleeping. Dakota had been up when I was texting her at midnight and tended to be a night owl anyway. Leah might be at work at the diner where she served breakfast to tourists.

Sully was miraculously still asleep. I checked to make sure he was still breathing, which he was. I tiptoed to the door, carefully pulling it open so it didn't squeak. Then I tiptoed down the hallway, which was all of about three feet, hoping I could get some water without Maddox hearing me. He didn't have to leave for the shop for another hour, so I was hoping to escape like a total coward before he woke up.

But my head was in the fridge reaching for my water bottle when I felt a very large, very masculine hand slide across my ass. I stood up so fast I hit my head on the top of the refrigerator. "Oh, shit!"

"Sorry, didn't mean to scare you." Maddox leaned against the counter, looking sleepy and sexy.

And naked. Very, very naked.

In the light of day, his body was even more of a wonder to me than it had been the night before. So much hardness.

"I thought you'd still be sleeping." I held up my reusable water bottle I kept chilling in the fridge. "I was thirsty."

"Me too." He took the bottle from me and took a long sip. "Ah. Thanks."

He had me trapped between the open refrigerator and the wall. "Excuse me." I gestured that I needed to get past him.

Maddox shifted about one inch. There was no way I could get by him without touching him. He didn't look like he was doing it on purpose. He looked like he was too sleepy to move much. But I was starting to realize that Maddox didn't do much of anything without a purpose.

He tried to hand me the water bottle back but I said, "Keep it. I'm going to meet my friends at the coffee shop in an hour. I'm going to jump in the shower now." You know, wash the smell of sex off of me. "I hope Sully wakes up soon. But not too soon." I gave a nervous laugh.

I *was* nervous. The kitchen was cozy, he was naked. I couldn't help but think about how good he'd been with his tongue, and how amazing it had felt to have his thick cock inside me. I'd missed sex in general and that had been great sex. I couldn't ask for a better way to break my celibacy streak. Yet I didn't know what the hell was supposed to happen now though. I had zero experience with this situation.

"If he's still sleeping, I can hang around until he's up, then bring him to you at the coffee shop."

"Aren't you going to Rebel Ink today?" I asked.

"We're doing late afternoon to late night. We're filming a birthday segment for Travis. I need to be there at four. I probably won't be home until two or three in the morning."

"Oh, okay. Fun." I was torn between wanting him home that night and being relieved I didn't have to have an accurate moment wondering if we were having sex again or not. "Are you sure you don't want to go back to bed, then?"

He shook his head and gave me a smile. "I can't sleep. Keep thinking about the way you feel underneath me."

My nipples hardened, which was ridiculous since they hadn't even been in play the night before. My mouth grew hot and I fought with everything inside me not to look down and see if he had a hard cock. Even with the open refrigerator blasting cold air on my backside, I was still feeling very warm.

I failed miserably. I looked down. Yep. Big dick.

Clearing my throat, I nodded. "It was definitely nice."

"Nice? Fuck nice." Maddox slid his hand around my waist. "If you thought it was just nice, I need another turn up to bat. I want a home run."

He'd already hit one but I was trying to stay cool. Which for me was damn near impossible. I felt nervous, but I also felt giddy and ecstatic that he had so easily found all my buttons and had pushed them so thoroughly. I wanted to twirl and laugh and grin, but at the same time panic because this was all wrong. Such a bad idea.

So being cool was not easy for me.

"I'm just trying to figure out how my sex life has become a sports metaphor," I said, in all seriousness.

He laughed softly. Pulling me against him, he dropped his gaze to my mouth. "You want straight talk?"

"I'm confused enough that yes, that would be very welcome." That was the complete and honest truth. I was super confused about what was happening and how to act.

"I want to fuck you this afternoon before I leave since I won't be home until late tonight. Is that straightforward enough?"

Um, yes. Everything down south went wet. I nodded. "That was very clear, thank you.

"You're welcome. What time does Sully nap?"

"One."

"Perfect." He let me go and shifted out of my way. "It's a date."

"THAT'S NOT A DATE," I said to Felicia, leaning forward to get closer to her. "That's a sex appointment. Oh my God, what am I doing?" I groaned. "This is so bad."

Felicia shook her head. "I thought you weren't going to shag your nanny. What happened?"

I pressed my hands against my hot cheeks. It might be November but I was boiling from the inside out. "I feel like this coffee shop needs to turn their heat down." I sipped my chai tea. "I went out with Dakota's friend and apparently, the way she sold this blind date to him was to tell him I was thirsty for dick. He showed up fully prepared to have sex within like the first twenty minutes. He didn't even offer to buy me a drink. So I came home super early and super annoyed and was telling Maddox about it and… I don't know." I didn't. Somewhere in that brief conversation the night before in the kitchen I might have told him I really, really wanted to have sex. "It was an accident."

Isla raised her eyebrows skeptically. She was wearing a thick knit scarf and she fiddled with it. "One, it's not hot in here. People keep opening the door and blasting us with cold air. Two, you cannot call sex an accident. An accident is when Leah got hit by a cab and rolled her ankle. Taking your clothes off and putting some guy's peen in your mouth is not in the same category."

"Ew! Why are you making it sound so gross?" I was offended by her attitude.

She laughed. "I just think you should take responsibility. You wanted to, you did. Just own it, Savannah."

"Fine! I did. I wanted to and I did. There. Are you happy? And it was good and I want more and he wants more and now what? That is what I'm asking. Now what?" I realized my voice had gotten too loud. A man in his early twenties was working on his laptop. He glanced at me.

I lowered my voice to a dramatic whisper. "Now what the actual hell am I supposed to do?"

"You can stop acting like you opened a portal to disaster with your vagina and just calm down. Let's start there." Isla gave me a grin.

My jaw dropped. "I kind of hate you right now."

"I guess I'm just failing to see the crisis."

Leave it to Isla to not indulge my hysteria. I was about to explain to her why this was a legitimate dilemma when the door to the shop opened and I saw it was Maddox entering. Sully was strapped to his broad chest in a baby carrier. It was a beautiful sight—like porn for women. A hot tattooed man in a leather jacket with a baby strapped to him. It was a walking fantasy. It was a meme. It was ovulation inspiring.

I waved to him. He waved back.

Isla swiveled to see who had entered. Felicia was next to me and could already see Maddox. "He's fucking brilliant," she said.

When Isla turned back to face us, her eyes were wide. "It's not like you stood a chance," she said, her voice low. "I know you showed us his pic but the baby just adds that extra layer of hot."

"I totally agree." I stood up as Maddox approached the table. Sully had spotted me and was making happy squealing sounds, pumping his arms and kicking Maddox in the gut. "Hi, baby." I bent down a little and gave him a kiss on his plump cheek.

Then I straightened and looked up at Maddox. "Thanks for

bringing him." I gestured behind me. "These are my friends Isla and Felicia. This is Maddox."

Did I say my friend? My nanny? Steven's best friend? My brand-new lover? I decided it was better not to give it a label.

"It's a pleasure," Felicia said.

"We've heard so much about you," Isla said. "So much."

That wasn't obvious or anything. Maddox gave me a questioning look but I just shrugged.

"It's great to finally meet Savannah's friends," he said.

"Do you want to grab a coffee and join us?" Felicia asked him.

"Sure, for a couple of minutes, then I'll leave you to your girl time."

"Want me to take Sully?" I asked.

He waved me off with his inked hand, before giving Sully's hair a stroke. "After I order is fine."

I watched him stroll to the counter, confident, casual. Tight ass in dark jeans. The cashier at the register was eyeing him like she'd love a crack at him, baby or not. Maybe because of the baby for all I knew.

"You only have one option," Isla said urgently.

"What?"

"Shh! He's coming back," Felicia said.

When in the history of Brooklyn had anyone ever gotten a coffee that fast? That had been thirty freaking seconds. I needed to hear my one and only option.

"I forgot my wallet," he said, patting his pants like it was going to magically appear. "I'm not thinking straight today. Probably stayed up too late last night."

I scrambled for my purse, praying he didn't say any more than that. "Here, I've got it."

"That's okay. I can skip the coffee."

"No, I insist. You're being really… helpful," I finished lamely. I handed him a ten. "I think we could both stand to wake up." I gave him a pointed look.

He didn't take the hint. Instead he just took the money and reached out and tugged the end of my hair in what felt like a very brother-like move. "You're the best."

As he went back to the counter, Felicia sucked her iced coffee so hard it made slurping sounds.

Isla shook her head a little. "We need to talk about this after he leaves."

We did. Though I didn't know what there was to say other than what I'd already texted them earlier—help. I needed serious help.

Maddox didn't seem at a loss for words. He returned to the table with a coffee held far away from his body so Sully couldn't grab at it or kick it. He set it down in the center of the table and took the seat next to Isla, grabbing Sully's legs and putting him in a sitting position as he lowered himself. The man knew his way around a baby. Every day he proved that to me in a dozen ways.

It was a typical Brooklyn coffee shop. Lots of wood, exposed brick, and industrial accents. There was a living wall of succulents with club chairs in front of it. I frequented it often because it was so close to my apartment but I hadn't established any sort of rapport with the staff because it seemed like they were always changing. Now the cashier who had helped Maddox strolled by with a rag in her hand to wipe the table next to us. She gave me a dirty look before eyeing Maddox with definite lust.

I felt so instantly territorial it alarmed me. *Friends with benefits. Repeat after me, Savannah Prescott. Fucking friends with benefits. Fucking friends. Or friends that were fucking, if you will. Nothing more.*

My thoughts were wandering off in various directions while Maddox was making conversation with my friends.

"I hear you're a chef," he said to Isla.

Had I told him that? God, the man paid attention. I didn't even remember saying that.

They chatted about the restaurant she was at, and he admitted to not liking to cook. He asked Felicia about her business and in turn they asked him about the tattoo shop and the show. I just listened, appreciating the mental break, and made faces at my son.

Until Maddox changed the subject. "Did Savannah tell you her date was a bust?"

I sat up straighter. "Oh, geez, let's not talk about that."

"Total bust. It sounds like there was some miscommunication," Isla said, completely ignoring me. "Like this guy thought she just wanted a bangfest and she didn't."

Really subtle. Not. I kicked her under the table. She totally ignored me and sipped her latte.

"With her next couple of setups we need to make sure the goal is clear," Isla continued. "She's looking for a relationship."

"Some guys are going to assume sex no matter what," Maddox said. "But yeah, it definitely sounds like a few DMs could have cleared that up ahead of time."

"You guys know I'm sitting here, right?"

No one really acknowledged my comment.

"I've been talking to this guy as Savannah," Felicia said, swiping through her phone. She showed a picture to Maddox. "What do you think?"

"He's not bad," Maddox said, even as he popped Sully's pacifier back in his mouth when he started fussing. "He looks quite a bit older than Savannah, though."

"He's forty-two. I figured that might be a better choice for a single mom."

What was happening? Why was Maddox discussing my dating life with my friends?

It was like the night before hadn't even happened. Which it most definitely had. Lots of tongue. Lots of body contact for an extended period of time.

"I don't think age has anything to do with parenting skills," Maddox said. "Has he been married before? Does he know how to compromise?"

"Oh, I should ask him that," Felicia said. She started typing. "Have you ever been married? For how long?"

Stunned from the conversation I finally realized what exactly Felicia had said she'd been doing.

"Wait a minute. You're talking to him as *me*?"

"You said I could," Felicia protested.

She was right. I had. But now it seemed bizarre. Or maybe it was just because Maddox was sitting there. Maybe if Maddox didn't exist I would find it highly entertaining to see how Felicia would pretend to be me. She was definitely more dry than I was.

"Then can I at least see his picture since everyone else has?" I held my hand out.

She started to give me her phone, but then she held it back. "Don't say anything off-putting."

I eyed her. "Why would I do that?"

"Just be engaging. He seems very nice."

"Maybe you should date him, Felicia," Isla said.

My thoughts exactly.

"Don't be silly. I picked him for Savannah. He thinks he's talking to a hot redhead, not a sallow Brit."

"I don't even know what sallow means," I told her, "but you're definitely a catch so don't downplay yourself." Felicia had big expressive eyes and cheekbones to die for.

She just shrugged. "I picked him for you," she repeated.

I looked at his picture. He appeared to be fit, but not super muscular. He had a pleasant smile, and wasn't fighting that his hair was graying at the temples. "He does look like a nice guy." I didn't have any burning desire to date him, but I wouldn't object.

I handed her the phone back and added, "But we all know my track record with men."

"Did Savannah tell you she has appalling taste in men?" Isla asked Maddox, sounding very cheerful about the whole thing.

"She did," he said, giving me a grin that unnerved me. "And she agreed to let me pick her fifth first date."

"Oh, she did, did she?" Isla said. "Interesting. So who would you choose for Savannah?"

I shifted on my seat, not wanting to hear this answer. This was already awkward.

"Someone totally unexpected. I'm still working out the details." Maddox started to undo the arms straps on the carrier. "Now I should head out and leave you to hang out."

I took Sully automatically and Maddox slipped the straps up onto my arm. He clicked the carrier in place as I dropped a kiss on Sully's downy head. "Thanks, Mad."

"See you later. One o'clock, remember?" He gave me a smoldering, intense, lust-filled gaze that had me blooming with heat.

He stood up as I nodded. "Absolutely. Yeppers. One o'clock it is." I gave an excited giggle and then hated myself for it. I couldn't help it though. The thought of more sex made me giddy.

Maddox gave me a smile, like he knew he made me ridiculous. He took Sully's hand and gave himself a high five with it. "Bye, kiddo." He waved to Felicia and Isla. "It was really good to meet you. Savannah is lucky to have such great friends."

Then he left with his coffee and I sat there in a haze of sexual want and general confusion.

"Well." Felicia turned and watched him leave. When the door shut behind him she said, "Remind me again why you can't just date him? Because I think he is quite the catch."

"I'm not disputing that," I said. "But he's ridiculously young. He's not marriage material. He also lives in Stroudsburg normally and is totally not my type. Do you see all those tattoos? Besides, he doesn't want to date me. You heard him discussing my love life like he's one of the girls."

"I would not say he sounded like one of the girls," Isla said. "Get real, Savannah. But I agree that while he clearly is awesome with your son, there is nothing there to indicate he wants a relationship with you."

That stung a little. Yes, she was agreeing with me, but I hadn't realized until that moment that maybe I wanted them to argue with me. To tell me to explore what it could be with Maddox beyond sex. "Exactly," I said, before lifting my coffee to my lips. My voice had wobbled a little.

"I know I'm the last woman on the planet to ask dating advice from, considering I never date these days, but I don't know that I agree with Isla. If you want to date him, shouldn't you at least try to see what might be there?"

"I don't want to date him," I said and I meant that emphatically. "Because if I date him, I'll fall in love with him, and there is no future in that. I'll wind up with a broken heart, I'll break my son's heart, and I will waste valuable years I could have spent finding a forever guy."

That put me back on solid footing. Eye on the prize. "Even if Maddox wants to date now, in a year he'll realize he's way too young for all the responsibility of dating a mom. He has half of his twenties still to be a selfish single guy. With a big dick, I might add. That is something that frankly should be shared with the women of New York City."

I didn't like anything I was saying, but it was the truth. I would fall in love with him. I could see that. Who wouldn't? Well, maybe women who could keep their emotions in check but that woman was not me.

"Which brings us back to my original statement," Isla said. "You only have one option."

"Right. What is that?" Felicia asked.

I was almost scared to hear what she was going to say. "Lay it on me."

"You have to continue with the four first dates. Two down, but you still have two to go. And now you have Maddox in on the action providing you with a fifth date. It's the only way you can continue to have sex with him and yet hold him at some kind of a distance. Or rather, keep yourself at a distance."

I had decidedly less enthusiasm for the project than I'd had a few weeks earlier but I knew she was right. "I agree. I have to see this through. It's a numbers game. If I want to find my Prince Charming I have to just keep dating. I might even need a round two."

"Think of it this way," Isla said. "Hanging out and hooking up with Maddox makes you way less desperate on these dates. You're coming from a power position. You have a great job, an adorable child, and you're getting your sex needs met by a guy you trust. You don't need anything from these guys, so if they suck, you just move on."

She was right. "Sometimes you are very smart," I told her.

"Sometimes? Try all the time." She gave me a grin. "Now let's see if Felicia's guy has answered her/you."

"He has," Felicia said. "He was married for five years but his wife died ten years ago." She made a sympathetic face. "That's so tragic."

"A widower. Wow. And he hasn't been married since? He must have really loved her." I felt myself softening to this guy.

"Oh, God, here we go," Isla said. "How do you know he isn't lying?"

"How do you know he isn't telling the truth?" I countered.

She sighed. "I suppose suggesting that he's probably still married and looking for side ass isn't going to go over well with either of you?"

"No," we both said simultaneously.

Isla sighed again, this time even more pronounced and dramatic. "You asked me to save you from yourself and I'm pretty sure it's a lost cause."

She was probably right. "I believe in love, you grump. You're right. In that way, I am a lost cause."

Nothing was going to change that. One day I would have my perfect rom-com love story.

If I could prevent myself from falling for my brother's best friend in the meantime.

WALKING BACK to the apartment after leaving Sully with Savannah, I called Steve. "Hey, what's up?" I said as a greeting when he answered.

"Is this important?" he said, sounding tired and like his phone was right against his face. "Because I have a friend over."

I knew what that meant. He was still in bed and had a girl with him. "Anyone I know?"

I paused at the corner, debating whether I wanted to return to the apartment or not. I decided to go change, then hit the gym. Or at the very least go running in the park. I had a ton of pent-up energy that I needed to get out. The conversation in the coffee shop had jacked me up and I couldn't exactly talk to my best friend about why it was bothering me.

"Uh, I don't think so. We met last night at the Tavern. Say hi, Kelsey."

I heard a female voice pipe up in the background. "Hi, Kelsey."

That actually made me laugh. "Nice." The wind had kicked up and it felt good on my face. I spotted a garbage can and pitched my now-cold coffee remnants. "I just met a couple of Savannah's friends. They seem cool."

"Are they hot?"

That made me roll my eyes. "You're a dick to even ask that when you have a *friend* next to you."

"She went to the bathroom. And you didn't answer my question."

I thought about Isla, who seemed like a badass. Pretty, but prickly. Felicia was attractive, but she shrank into herself a little. Neither were my type and neither were Steve's type. But that wasn't even the point. "You can't hit on your sister's friends, so it doesn't matter."

"Why not?"

"Picture me hitting on Savannah." Yeah, I was testing the waters. I couldn't help it. I felt agitated and pissed off at the idea of Savannah going out with other men.

"Fuck that, bro. I'd kill you."

I had figured as much. "She feels the same way about you and her friends."

I was in dicey territory but I needed advice, and Jana was too enthusiastic. Too into the whole fantasy of me and Savannah, not into anything practical. I needed someone who wasn't all about the relationship fantasy to be realistic with me. "I met this chick," I said. "I'm really into her and we hooked up last night."

"Sounds good so far."

"She's talking to other guys, making plans with them. I don't want that. What do I do now? I got greedy and had sex with her and now I think I did everything backwards, you know?" I hadn't been able to resist her standing in the kitchen lamenting the lack of sex in her life. I'd gone for it and now I was sitting in fucking coffee shops helping her friends plan dates for her.

Not smart.

"Tell her you want to lock her in."

"It's too soon for that. She'll tell me to go fuck myself." She would think I was crazy, no question about it.

"Then date other girls. She's dating other guys. Maybe she'll see you with another chick and freak."

"Isn't that just game playing?"

"Of course it is. Those are your three choices—tell her, do what she's doing, or walk away. That's all you can do."

"I don't like any of those choices."

"You're talking to the wrong guy. Let me ask Kelsey." He rustled around and I heard him yell, "Hey, Kels. My buddy needs advice on women."

Oh, great. Now I was the loser who needed Jana, Steven, and some girl I'd never met to try to fix my love life. "Don't put her on the phone. I'm serious."

"Hey, this is Kelsey," a breathy voice said, like she'd jumped or fallen onto the bed. "Who's this?"

I rubbed my temples and looked up at the sky. It was tempting to give her a fake name. "This is Maddox."

"Nice to meet you. Give me the rundown."

I told her as briefly as possible what I'd told Steven.

"Was it pity sex?" she asked. "Did she feel sorry for you?"

"What?" For fuck's sake. "No. Of course not."

"Send me a selfie so I know for sure."

"No," I said flatly, insulted. "She did not have sex with me because she feels sorry for me. By the way, no one should ever do that with anyone. It's weird."

"That's why I came home with Steven," she said.

"Hey!" he said in the background.

The teasing tone of her voice clued me in that she was joking, so I did actually laugh. Kelsey had a decent sense of humor. "I can see that, but honestly, you should make him work harder for any future hookups."

"I'm never seeing him again," she said cheerfully.

Then she squealed in delight and there was lots of muffled sounds that made it clear he had grabbed her and they were no longer interested in talking to me in any way.

I ended the call.

I texted Jana.

Had sex with Savannah. I think I fucked up the almost kiss ten times but don't step.

She answered right away.

HOLY SHIT.

What do I do now?

Hang on. I'm sending you a list of movies where they hook up before they declare their feelings for each other.

That made me roll my eyes. Yet at the same time it didn't stop me from staring at my phone waiting for her answer.

Watch Friends with Benefits and The Proposal. NOW.

I looked up both and decided Friends with Benefits might be too close to reality.

After changing I went to the gym and ran on the treadmill, watching The Proposal with Ryan Reynolds and Sandra Bullock on my phone with my earbuds in.

WWRRD.

Fuck.

Chapter 9

MADDOX HADN'T BEEN in the apartment when I got back and he didn't show up until almost one on the dot. It was making me nervous. I had never had a relationship like this. I'd barely had hookups, never a friends-with-benefits situation, and definitely never with a roommate.

I was putting Sully down for his nap when I heard Maddox open the front door and come in. After turning on my tablet to soft nursery rhyme music I left the room and gently pulled the door shut.

He was taking off his running shoes and was wearing athletic shorts and a T-shirt.

"Hi," I said, keeping my voice low. "Did you have a good workout?"

He nodded. "I love the way it clears my head."

Something about his tone gave me pause. Was he going to say we shouldn't have sex anymore? That would be both probably a wise thing and a terrible thing.

But Maddox didn't say anything of the kind and I was being weird and panicky.

"I wish I felt that way about exercise," I said, running my hand over my stomach without meaning to. "I've always felt like I was being tortured. I really should force myself to get back to it though."

Yet another thing Maddox and I didn't have in common. We really had different personalities.

"You're a mom. You're really busy," he said, before stripping off his shirt and tossing it and his phone on the end table. "If you hate working out, it shouldn't be a priority. Focus more on healthy eating and getting a good night's sleep."

I was distracted by his damp, now naked chest.

Then his shorts and boxer briefs came off without any warning.

An involuntary gasp came out of my mouth.

"I need to shower," he said, moving in close to me.

He brushed my hair back and then fisted it a little in a move that both startled and aroused me.

"Take your clothes off," he said. "I want you in the shower with me."

"It's a small shower," I protested, for no apparent reason. "We won't fit." The minute the words came out of my mouth I regretted them. If this was all about sex, I should embrace it fully. In another six weeks he'd be gone and I would be kicking myself for missed opportunities.

"The water will cover up the sound of you screaming my name."

The way he flipped the switch was amazing to me. One minute he was Mr. Nice Guy, nanny extraordinaire. The next he was alpha male, dirty talking and demanding. I liked both. Right now, I was really fond of Dirty Talker. It made me less nervous. There was no time to be weird when I was hot for him and willing to do whatever he wanted.

"I see," I said. "Sounds like you have a plan."

His hands were on my hips. Maddox kissed me, teasing at my lips with his tongue. Then he lowered his palms to my ass and ground me against him. Before I could even enjoy the impact of my body pressed against his cock, he pivoted me and gave my ass a playful, but not entirely gentle, slap.

"Get moving, Savannah. We're on a schedule."

I obeyed, because who the hell wouldn't? I walked to the bathroom, peeling my shirt off as I went. As he closed the door and we crowded into the small space, I tried not to eye the shower stall skeptically. It wasn't a bathtub-shower combination. It was a full shower stall insert, with a cruddy plastic floor pan. It was smaller than a tub would be. At best one and a half people could fit in it. Or Maddox and Sully.

Normally I bathed Sully in the bathroom sink because it was easier and brighter. The lighting in the shower sucked.

I turned to suggest maybe this was going to be a fail when Maddox reached past me and turned the shower on. Then he stripped me out of my joggers with one sharp downward motion. "Oh!" I said. He clearly had no intention of abandoning the project.

I never saw myself as a woman who fell for the muscles, but I had to admit, I didn't hate touching Maddox. He was a whole different level of hard compared to previous men I'd been with and it was fascinating and sexy as hell. As he kissed me I greedily ran my fingers across his chest and abs. I went further and slide my hand over his cock. He gave a low growl.

Liking the sound of that, I squeezed at the base of his shaft.

"Savannah," he said. "You are so fucking hot, do you know that?"

I didn't answer, but just pulled my hand away, and watched him as I drew my tongue across my fingers to slick them up. His eyes darkened. I returned to his thick erection and worked my hand up and down, enjoying the way he stood still, tense, lacing his fingers through mine on my free hand.

"You still haven't told me what any of your tattoos mean," I said, scanning his body. An eagle here, a skull there, a complex roping of what looked like metal chains. He had art everywhere, and I was still amazed by the amount of time and patience and meaning that had clearly gone into it.

"I'm still here for awhile. We have plenty of time."

I gripped him harder at that, for reasons I didn't want to look too closely at.

Maddox sucked in a sharp breath, then gripped my wrist. He pulled me off of him, and pressed my hands back onto the vanity countertop.

Before I could process his plan, he was down on his knees, and still holding my hands hostage, he buried his tongue inside me.

"Mad, oh, God," I said, realizing a fraction too late that my voice was loud and keening. Hopefully the shower had drowned it out because there was no way I could manage silent sex, not with him working me like he was.

He was deep inside me and I felt surrounded by his broad shoulders, his strong arms. I wanted to grab on to his dark hair and pull him away because it was so intense, but he had me pinned so I couldn't move. It only took a few seconds before I was crying out with a hot, fast orgasm.

Then he released me while I stood there, legs shaking, panting hard, inner thighs quivering. They were freaking quivering and I was thinking that might have been my fastest zero to orgasm in recorded history.

But before I could speak or process or reach for him, he had a condom on and lifted me up and onto the sink. He lifted my legs onto his hips and he lifted me back off the sink and right onto his cock.

He was right. I screamed his name.

Somehow, he was holding up all my weight and still managing to lift me up and down onto him. It was a move I'd never experienced because how many men have the thigh and core strength for that? None I'd ever dated.

It was sexy as hell to have gravity dropping me fully on him so he was embedded deep inside me. I'd never felt so *taken*. All I could do was grip his shoulders tightly and just try not to drown in the pleasure.

"Does that feel good?" he asked, eyes locked with mine. "Tell me how that feels, Savannah."

"It feels amazing." I tossed my hair back, wanting him to react.

He did. He made that sound in the back of his throat that I loved.

"How does that feel to you, Maddox?" I was probably playing with fire asking him that.

"How does that feel?" He was barely even breathing hard as

he continued to move me on him. "Like victory. Like winning. Like hot, sexy slickness clamping down on me. Like nothing else matters except this. Right here. Right now."

The more he spoke, words washing over me, the closer and closer I came to the edge. His voice was low, hypnotic, sensual.

"Like you have the tightest, sweetest pussy ever."

Maddox turned and pushed me against the wall. Then he pounded into me, hard, mouth just hovering over mine, but not touching. In a hot cocoon of steam from the shower and his hard, damp body, I let go and embraced my orgasm, crying out desperately.

He did the same and then we were staring at each other, panting, still joined together. I would have brushed a stray hair out of my face but I couldn't let go of him. My whole body felt like if I tried to move I would fall. I was shaken, shoulders and face burning.

Without speaking, Maddox set me down carefully and turned away, removing the condom. I wanted to touch him. I trailed my fingertips over the breadth of his back. My legs were still weak and I wrapped my arms around him, leaning against him for support.

But he stepped away from me. "Get in the shower," he said.

He wasn't looking at me, but his tone was both commanding and sensual. I shivered, rubbing my arms. I had no idea what he still had in store for me, but I was looking forward to it. I slipped my bra off and stepped in.

"Aren't you coming in?" I asked when he didn't join me. He was leaning on the countertop, head hung so that I couldn't see his expression.

Maddox bent over and drank straight from the faucet. "Of course." Then he stood up and gave me a smile. "I'm going to be inside you until Sullivan wakes up. Just so you know."

I returned his smile. "I'm counting on it."

. . .

"WHAT'S UP WITH YOU?" Jana asked, nudging me as she went past my station. "Did you do your homework?"

I was drawing a sketch for an upcoming appointment and trying not to think about Savannah. I was failing miserably at that. We'd just had sex three times in twenty-four hours. It wasn't likely I was shaking that anytime soon.

"Nothing's up with me. I watched The Proposal but I'm not sure what I was supposed to see other than Betty White is awesome and I already knew that." I didn't look up from my sketch. A midnight client wanted a pirate ship on his forearm, which didn't give me a lot of space for the amount of shading and detail I wanted to give him. "What's up with you?"

"Nothing much. I just met someone and I'm probably going to marry her on my next day off."

That had me lifting my head. "You move fast. Congratulations."

She rolled her eyes. "You're impossible to unnerve. It's very unnerving."

"Who am I to judge if you fall in love at first sight?" I'd been hot for the same girl for a decade. No judgment from me, that was for damn sure.

"It's definitely lust at first sight. I was kidding about getting married. But you never know, right? All I know is she's hot and I want to spend every second I'm not working with her. That's a start, right?"

"It is. What's her name?"

Jana was wearing shorts and black socks that came up to her knees and a Sailor Moon hoodie. She leaned against my chair and propped her head up with her chin. "It's Brandy. Would it be weird if I tattooed her name on my finger so I can have her inside me when I diddle myself?"

I almost dropped my pencil. I started laughing. Jana was definitely one of a kind. "I get the concept in theory, but don't you think she'll find that just a little stalker-ish at this point in your what… one-week-old relationship?"

"You're so practical it's gross," she complained. "Oh, hey," she said. "Can I help you?"

"I have an appointment with Maddox Malone," a decidedly female voice replied.

I turned and found a girl about my age standing there. She had dark hair and a retro pinup girl look. "Are you Maddox?" She stuck her hand out. "I'm Johnny."

So the pirate ship was going on a woman? Shit. Now I was really out of room. A glance at her arms showed they were slim. "Oh, hi, nice to meet you." I stood up and took her outstretched hand. "I was just given the name John, so I was expecting a guy. Which you're obviously not. I shouldn't have made an assumption."

She laughed. "Nope. Not a guy. Not even close. Though I do like guys."

I recognized that tone. Mild flirtation. I cleared my throat and let go of her hand. I wanted to stay professional.

Jana was suddenly up next to me in a way she never was. She was practically climbing up my leg. I gave her a "what the fuck" look.

"We're hanging out later, remember?" she said.

We had exactly zero plans to hang out later but she was trying to tell me something, that was obvious. I cautiously nodded. "Sure," I said.

Then Jana kissed me, so fast it barely happened. I was so shocked I didn't pull away. Besides, it was over in a blink. Considering I knew she had no sexual feelings for me and that she was madly in love with a woman she'd just met, I figured she had to think she was protecting me from the evil clutches of Johnny, a woman we'd met two seconds ago.

Which was insane.

I could handle myself if and when Johnny wanted to flirt, but mostly, I thought she was probably just being friendly. You know, in the last thirty seconds. I watched Jana leave, tossing her long hair back off her shoulder.

"Your girlfriend is cute," Johnny said as I gestured for her to have a seat.

"She's lost her mind," I said. I debated telling the truth or not, but decided I didn't care enough to correct the assumption.

"I think she thought I was going to hit on you. Which I still might," she said, giving me a sassy grin. "You're not bad to look at."

"Thanks. And I could see how you could inspire jealousy." What? Jana wasn't my girlfriend and Savannah was dating random guys. I could give a compliment back to someone.

"Is she going to come over here and try to girl fight me?" Johnny sat down in her tight jeans and leaned back into the chair, her tits spilling out of her sweater.

"Jana is scrappy. You never know." I showed her my sketch. "Now, about your tat. I was told pirate ship but I thought you were a dude, so I may be way off base here."

She glanced at it and nodded. "I want something way more feminine." She took her sweater off and started showing me her existing tattoos. Which wasn't that outrageous in a shop. There was a lot of necessary nudity, and in this case, it would be important for me to see her current tats so I could stylistically tie her new one into the old.

The sad thing was, she had a great body. Her bra was sheer and I could see her nipples. And it did exactly nothing for me because I could have sworn I could still taste Savannah on my tongue.

I had gone too far with her.

And I wasn't sure how to bring myself back.

After Johnny left I went and found Jana. "Are you done for the night?"

She was cleaning her station. "Yes, why?"

"We're hanging out tonight, remember? According to you when you kissed me two hours ago." I crossed my arms over my chest and eyed her.

Anyone else would have the decency to look sheepish. Not Jana. She looked proud of herself. "I had to do something. That girl was a predator. I can't have you screwing up this thing with Savannah when we're on the cusp of a break through."

"I know how to deflect someone's interest in me," I said,

rolling my eyes. "I don't think you understand. I'm in love with Savannah. I want to marry her and make more babies with her. I'm not susceptible to *anyone* else."

Jana fanned herself. "Growl. I love it. I'm texting you a list." She was already on her phone, typing furiously.

"What kind of list?"

"Your rom-com moments. I feel like you're doing well in the confidant category but you stepped out of order with the sex. We need to recover." She looked up. "There. Promise me you'll do these things."

Curious, I pulled out my phone.

1. Eat ice cream with her
2. Take her ice skating
3. Go grocery shopping with her
4. Buy her a gift, something small
5. Dance with her at the engagement party

"WHY ICE SKATING?"

"Because it's November in New York City and everyone in every movie ever in the city in November or December goes ice skating at Rockefeller Center. She'll be eating out of your hand."

Since I'd been accused of being pragmatic and practical I decided I had nothing to lose by listening to her. "Fine. I'm on it. But this means I get to offer you a practical guide to Brandy, the new love of your life. And it starts with not tattooing her name anywhere on your body."

"Boo." Her nose wrinkled. "But I guess you've had worse ideas."

I laughed. "I never have bad ideas, what are you talking about?" Samuel walked past me, bouncing to the music playing overhead. "Samuel, do I have bad ideas?"

"No way, man. You're the guy to trust."

"See?" I gave Jana a smug look. "I'm practical and trustworthy. Some people appreciate that."

"Not people with vaginas."

There was no winning. "I would have done everything on that list on my own, by the way. Except for the ice skating. But everything else I would have done."

"Pfft."

Chapter 10

I STARED across the table at Michael, Felicia's choice for me. I was trying to focus. Apparently, Felicia had been talking to him quite a bit as me and I'd had to read through their dozens of messages to each other. I thought she might have taken the getting-to-know-him thing way too far. A few messages then a meet-up would have made more sense because now she had all this information about him and I was playing catch-up.

It made it feel more forced than it might have otherwise.

"You're even more beautiful in person than your picture," he said, smiling.

It was just as pleasant a smile as it had been when Felicia had showed me his profile. "Thank you," I said, crossing and uncrossing my legs. "You're a doctor, right? What specialty?"

He gave me a puzzled look. "Um, orthopedics. Sorry, I thought we talked about this. You mentioned your grandmother's hip replacement."

What the hell, Felicia? My cheeks went hot. "Right, of course. Duh. Mom brain." I pointed to my head, feeling like an idiot.

"Oh, right, sure. I understand. Besides, I imagine you talk to a lot of guys, not just me."

He didn't say it in a way that was an accusation but it still made me uncomfortable. "I wouldn't say that." I wouldn't. I wasn't talking to any guys except for Maddox.

"Dating has changed so much in the last ten years. It's hard to get to know someone when everyone is just swiping like crazy." Michael lifted his bourbon and gestured to me. "That's why I appreciate how much you've been willing to chat with me before meeting."

Death to Felicia. I was going to murder her. I felt like a fraud. I was Jennifer Lopez in Maid in Manhattan bullshitting her way through a gala. Without a beautiful borrowed gown.

"It must be hard for you to date with your schedule. I'm sure you're a very busy man."

We were in a very nice restaurant—in Brooklyn, because he was considerate—with a hushed, intimate atmosphere and I really wanted to focus on Michael. I wanted to like him. Because he seemed like an actual nice guy.

But all I could think about was Maddox burying his tongue inside me.

It made for a very distracted dinner date.

"Ten years ago that was true. But now I have more flexibility at work because of the heights I've reached in the hierarchy. Ironic, because now I have more time and no special person in my life." He smiled. "Hence, the torture of dating apps."

I laughed. "Everyone's doing it. It can't be that awful or we'd all stop collectively." I eyed the waitress passing me with a glass of red wine. "I haven't had a glass of wine in fifteen months. Is it terrible that I just really, really want one?"

"I'm sure you could have a sip or two. Just pump your milk for the next twelve hours." He gave me a wink. "I'm a doctor. I know what I'm talking about."

It should be reassuring. He was comfortable with my mom status. With breast milk. Not all men would be. But I was feeling like Michael would be a lovely friend and companion, but not a boyfriend. Which was super premature. I'd been with him for all of twenty minutes.

"My mom guilt is too strong. But that first glass after weaning my son is going to be a beautiful moment."

He sipped his bourbon. "By the way, does our age difference bother you in any way?"

Did it? I honestly wasn't sure. It was a little bit like being on a date with one of my dad's golfing buddies. Maybe that had more to do with his personality than his age, though. He was very polite, and maybe I wanted something more fluid, natural.

Like me and Maddox.

I mentally kicked myself and said, "No, of course not."

"I was leery about putting it out there I was interested in younger women, because I don't want to be a creepy older guy, but I really want a family. After my wife passed away I put my head down and just worked. Then one day I woke up and I was forty." He shrugged. "That's selfish, I know it is, because women can't do the same thing. But I want to be honest."

"Age is just a number," I said, even as I wondered if I believed that. If I did, I wouldn't point to Maddox's age as a reason I couldn't be with him. It clearly did matter to me.

I stared across the table at Michael and realized I had exactly zero clue what the hell I was doing in my dating life.

"TASTE THIS," I said, lifting my spoon to Maddox's lips as he held Sully. "Does it need more salt?"

He obediently opened his mouth and took the pesto. He shook his head. "No, it's fine. It's good."

It was the night after my dinner with Michael and I was making dinner the way I normally did. Maddox and I had fallen into a routine. During the week, I made dinner, we hung out with the baby, talked, watched TV, put Sully down. Then had sex before I retreated to my bedroom. Everything about it was easy, unlike staring across the restaurant table at a stranger. Michael had texted me a very thoughtful "just wanted to make sure you got home okay" text the night before, which I'd answered because only a bitch wouldn't acknowledge that.

But then he had texted me again that afternoon and I hadn't responded. I wasn't feeling it, even though he was the stuff of rom-coms. He was "hold his umbrella in the rain for you" guy. And yet… no sparks.

I turned and my hip bumped Maddox's. Huh. What a shocker I wasn't into a perfectly polite stranger when I had a hot muscular tattoo artist/nanny giving it to me every night, right?

So ridiculous.

"Hey, I wanted to let you know in three weeks I need to go back home for the weekend. It's my mom's birthday."

"Okay, thanks for letting me know." Was that disappointment I felt? That I would lose a weekend with him? Isla was going to shake me if she found out my inner thoughts.

"Oh, and I got you some ice cream on my way home." Maddox wasn't looking at me. He was making faces at Sully, who kept reaching for his lips. Maddox pretended to eat Sully's fingers, making my son laugh.

I opened the fridge after stirring the pesto over the chicken I'd whipped up. There it was. Caramel Core ice cream. My favorite. "You're the best."

"I know." He ran his gaze over me.

I tried to ignore the fact that all he had to do was look at me and I melted like ice cream left out overnight. "Didn't you get some for yourself?"

"Nope. I'm off sugar. Need to stay in shape."

"Your shape is fine."

"You say that now but when a month goes by and I have a gut you're going to change your mind. Admit it, you like my body."

"I never said I didn't. But you're more than your body." I did mean that. Maddox was a good man.

"I'm just kidding. I work out for me. I like the way I feel when I'm pushing my body to perform."

"When did you start working out? I don't remember you looking like anything other than a standard lanky teenager."

"Seventeen. I wanted to be strong enough to really control a motorcycle and it just spiraled from there." He looked in the pan. "Are we ready to eat? I'll strap Sully into his seat."

"Ready." I dished up the food and brought it to my coffee table turned dining table. "It would be nice one day to have an actual table."

"That's hard in New York. Space is at a premium."

"Very. I don't see myself moving anytime soon either. Though I could get one of those tables that hangs on the wall and you take it down at mealtime."

"I'm not sure where you'd put it. Sully has taken over the living room with his stuff."

It was true. It was also true that it was nice to talk to someone about the everyday mundane stuff. Living alone with Sully had been different. Sure, I'd talked out loud to my son, but he couldn't weigh in on simple things like furniture placement. I was going to miss the companionship when Maddox was gone.

Yes, I was going to miss the sex, but we had become really good friends. "What are you getting your mom for her birthday?" I asked.

"Me. I'm coming home. That's her gift."

I laughed. "You can't be serious! That's sweet, but not a gift."

"You don't think I'm a gift?" He put his hand on his chest. "I'm mortally wounded."

"I don't know what you are," I told him honestly.

"Do you want me to tell you?" he asked.

Equally unnerved and amused, I shook my head. "No. I don't think so. Get us some plates."

"Let's go ice skating," Maddox said when we were sitting around my coffee table.

"What?" I asked, startled. "You want to go ice skating?"

"Yes. We did that once when we were kids, remember? Your mom took us into the city and we skated at Rockefeller Center."

That was a memory I'd totally forgotten about. I smiled. "Oh, yeah. I was about fourteen, I guess. I could barely skate because I was so worried my outfit wasn't cool enough for the city. Geez, what a horrible age." I shuddered. "I have a vague memory of arguing with Steven too, though I can't remember about what."

"He yanked your hat off your head and you fell trying to skate after him to get it back."

I made a face. "How could I forget that? I was so annoyed with him. All his little brother bullshit. Sometimes it was too much." But I remembered the rest of that story too. "You sat down on the ice with me and pretended like we'd done it on purpose so I wouldn't be as embarrassed." Smiling at him, I added, "You were a sweet little kid."

"Do you still see me as just your little brother's best friend?" he asked.

The question felt weighty. Important. Wetting my bottom lip with my tongue, I shook my head. "No. Of course not. I see you as my friend too."

His nostrils flared.

Our relationship blurred so many lines that sometimes I didn't know what to say to him. He was never short on words or actions. But I found myself feeling more than the words I'd spoken. We weren't just friends. We were friends and roommates and lovers.

Oh. My. God.

We were dating without dating.

"Friends with benefits," he said.

Right. Friends with benefits. "Exactly," I said, as if I had any clue what I was doing. Which I had none. Zero clues. Negative clues. Less than.

Thirty minutes later we were on the couch and Maddox was stealing my ice cream. "Hey! You said you're off sugar."

"It smells good." He licked my spoon and gave me a smile. "Sorry."

"Ice cream doesn't have a scent from three feet away." I took my spoon back. "You're not even remotely sorry."

"It's my reward for watching this movie with you."

All week I'd been running a Sandra Bullock marathon for Maddox. That night we were watching While You Were Sleeping.

"This is a great movie. You're going to love it. Because the guy she saves in the coma isn't the guy she ends up with."

Maddox threw his hands up. "What the hell? You just told me the ending! Now I don't need or want to watch it."

"I didn't tell you who she ends up with," I protested.

"How hard could it be to figure out? You suck at secrets. Admit it. You always sucked at secrets. Remember when your friend Jennifer made out with the janitor and you told everyone?"

"Because he was the janitor!" I protested. "That was gross."

"He was eighteen and so was she. They made out at the

bowling alley on a Friday night like three weeks after Jennifer's graduation."

"Semantics. It was still inappropriate." I checked to made sure Sully was content on his blanket on the floor and I paused the movie because we were missing a pivotal part.

"Fine. I'll give you that. Though I fault the school for hiring an eighteen-year-old. Bad move. Okay, so remember the time Steven was getting the latest Mario Kart game for Christmas and you told him and your mom didn't talk to you for two days?"

"That wasn't an intentional slip. We got a phone call on the house phone and I answered it and it was Luigi telling me my game would be ready for pickup on release day, so I turned and told everyone that. I didn't know it was a secret. I thought it was cool Luigi called us."

Maddox laughed. "That's so fifteen years ago, isn't it? Recordings from Luigi on the house phone."

"Yes, now be quiet and watch the movie."

"That you ruined," he said.

I stuck my tongue out at him.

My phone was on the cushion between us and it buzzed.

"The old guy is texting you," Maddox said.

It was Michael. "Stop it. He's not old. He's age appropriate."

"For my mom."

He had a point. "Don't hate. He wants to have children. I don't think it's strange he'd want to date younger."

"He can adopt a baby." Maddox picked up the remote. "So you're going out with him again? He's a two-timer?"

"I haven't decided yet."

"He's not getting any younger," he joked.

I laughed. "Shut up. That is ageism and totally unnecessary. Forty is the new thirty. Besides, you sat there in the coffee shop and gave him the thumbs-up. What's the issue now?"

"I don't have an issue. Just teasing you. Who's next up? Unless you're going out with Michael again."

"I don't know. Isla is dragging her feet. I don't think she's taking this seriously." I glanced at Michael's text. He was clearly trying to get a response. I was flattered he wanted to see me again.

"I don't think I should see Michael again. I'm not feeling it and he seems very nice, and eager. I don't want to lead him on."

"Then Isla better get on it with number four. I have my guy all picked out already."

Maddox had a guy picked out for me? I stared at him. "Who?"

"I'm not telling you. Unlike you, I can keep a secret."

I basically hated that answer. "Why does it have to be a secret?" I nudged his leg with my knee. "Come on, tell me."

"Because he's fifth. He only comes into play if three and four don't work out. No, I'm not telling you."

"Who wanted that rule?" Not me.

"You can't be dating someone and looking ahead, wondering if the next guy is better. That's not cool."

Okay, maybe he had a point. I could see that. "Fine. Does he work with you?" I asked, curious.

Maddox gave me a look. "I work with two guys. Why would I answer that question? Then you would know it was one or the other. I'm not an amateur, you know."

I made a sound of exasperation. I had thought this whole experiment was going to be so amazing and at the end I would find Prince Charming. So far, not the case. But I could honestly say only Yates Caldwell had been a frog. Or more like a shark. At least it hadn't been all horrible. But no Mr. Right either.

Sully was starting to fuss. He was working toward a good cry and I was comfortable on the couch. I felt lazy and very into my ice cream. "Can you get the baby?" I gave Maddox a pleading smile. "Please. Please. Please. Please. Please."

He laughed. "Oh my God. Stop. I'll get him. You're lucky you're pretty because you're also super annoying."

"Ice cream?" I asked, holding my spoon out for him.

Maddox put his mouth over the spoon and took the huge bite of ice cream. He shook his head like a dog. "Whew. Good stuff. It's like doing a shot of sugar."

Then he got off the couch and scooped Sully off the floor and straight up over his head. "Come here, little man. No fussing during movie night." He brought him to the couch and tucked him into the crook of his arm.

I held my hands out. "Can I have my baby?"

"No way. No work, no reward. I changed his last diaper too, so I get to sit with him."

"That feels like a scam. I did give birth to him."

He gave me a look. "You're pulling that card? Fine. I can't argue with that." He passed Sully over to me.

I took my son and looked down at his little face as he gave me a gummy smile. He made a cooing sound.

Then he reached his arms back out for Maddox.

"Hey!" I protested. "Traitor," I told Sully. I eyed Maddox. "You've turned my baby against me."

"He just likes talking about football and motorcycles with me."

I cuddled Sully in closer to my chest so he would forget that he wanted Maddox.

And so that I could forget I wanted Maddox.

I wondered if having him as a nanny and living with us was a mistake I never anticipated.

When he left I suspected it was going to break both Sully's and my hearts.

Because all joking aside, he *was* a gift. To me.

Chapter 11

"WHAT?" I stared at the producer of Rebel Ink, Mark, a guy in his fifties with a thick stomach and glasses. "Are you serious?"

"I'm serious. I'm sorry, but we really need to keep things interesting and draw in the viewers. You have the right look, but we need a storyline for you. Drama. If we can't come up with something we're going to have to replace you."

I was in his office at three in the morning after a long shift working and filming and I guess I wasn't totally surprised. Nor was I pissed. I was just… annoyed. You couldn't just be a fucking functional human being and keep your job? You had to be a dick or crazy? Apparently on reality TV you did. There was no point in arguing about it.

"What kind of storyline?"

"The most honest moment you've had was when you were talking about your mother being fifteen when she had you. We need more personal angles, like that." Mark was sitting on his desk, instead of behind it. He had his feet crossed at the ankle, arms over his chest, as he rubbed his chin.

"I don't have a sob story. My mom worked hard, got married, has a nice life."

"Then you need to be the flirt with clients or have a love triangle with Stella and Jana."

That made me laugh. "With Jana and Stella? How does that work?"

"Jana was clearly jealous of your client tonight. You could ask the client out, stir things up."

I wanted this job. More than I had realized. I really loved living in Brooklyn, working with other young tattoo artists. My thoughts had slowly been shifting from going back to Stroudsburg to staying. I sure in the hell didn't want to get bounced now.

If I had to leave the show now, I had to leave Savannah. I didn't want to give either one of them up. Not one minute sooner than I had to.

My thoughts churned, trying to find an angle. "I have an idea. Can I bring Jana in here so we can discuss it?"

"Sure. Call her in." Mark looked on the verge of being bored.

I yanked the door open. "Jana! Mark needs you in here."

She popped up from cleaning her station. "What? Why?" She came over and hovered in the doorway. "What's up?"

"Come in and close the door," Mark said.

Jana looked at me nervously. "Am I in trouble?"

"No, not at all," I said. "I'm in trouble and I need your help. Mark wants me to have a storyline. My storyline is us plotting for me to get the girl." I turned to Mark and explained the situation as quickly as I could. "Jana and I were talking outside one day and we danced around the topic but we could film the rest of the conversation like it happened then and edit it. We could film a couple of spots like, working backward."

"I love everything about this," Jana said.

"It's not a bad idea. This only works if you get the girl though in the end."

"Oh, I have her," I lied. "We're together. What if I ask my girlfriend and her baby to be on the show?" Savannah was not my girlfriend, but I could ask her to fake it. I was faking it as her boyfriend for her friend's upcoming engagement party. This could be the same thing.

Only it was going to be on TV. She'd never agree to that.

But at the same time, she was used to filming video spots for her own career, and she'd shown Sully in videos. I'd seen them.

Exposure was always good for someone who used social media as a platform. Maybe I could convince her if I asked her at the right moment.

Besides, this was a grand gesture, right? She loved that, and everything about me talking to a friend on a reality TV to plot how to win her was basically one of her movies.

In the end, maybe it would actually score points with her.

"You have a girlfriend?" Mark asked. "Why did I not know this?"

"It's brand new," I said. Slight exaggeration but I wasn't hurting anyone. "We live together." That was the truth. I pulled out my phone and showed him a picture I'd taken the week before of Savannah with Sully on the floor of the apartment. Her red hair was spilling across her face and she was laughing. Sully was staring up at her like she was a goddess.

"This isn't your kid?"

"No."

"There's your angle, too. Kid of a single mom dates single mom. Bring her in. We'll run with it and see how it plays."

I didn't want my life or Savannah to be an "angle." But at the same time, I didn't want to lose the gig.

"I'll talk to her," I said.

"Go back and look at the film and shoot those spots tomorrow. Make sure you wear exactly what you were wearing in the original segment."

"I hate being an outfit repeater," Jana said.

"So change after," I said. "Jana, you have to do this for me."

"Oh, I'm doing it. I never said I wasn't. This is insane and I love everything about it."

I *didn't* love it. But I was willing to do whatever I needed to so that I wouldn't lose my job and Savannah before I really even had her.

I KNEW PRECISELY when to talk to Savannah. Two days later while we were post-sex naked on the couch, panting and satisfied.

"God, I love nap-time," I told her. It was my favorite part of Saturdays.

She laughed and pushed on my chest. "I can't breathe."

I backed off and found the blanket on the back of the couch and pulled it over us. "I have an issue at work I want to talk to you about."

She turned onto her side and faced me. "What? Is everything okay?"

I laid it all out for her. Well. Not all of it. Just the end part, where I needed her to be my girlfriend.

"Oh, Mad… I don't know. I mean, I can pretend to be your girlfriend at the shop or a party or something, but on film? That's so dicey. Everyone will see it. My parents, Steven, your parents, your siblings. Is that a good idea?"

Considering I have every intention of convincing her to make a fake relationship real, I didn't think it was a big deal at all. But I had to be cool. "It's reality TV. Which is never reality. Everyone knows that."

"That is true."

She reached out and stroked my face in a gesture that was so sensual I felt my cock stirring to life again. "Maybe you'll have to persuade me in other ways."

"I can do that." I shifted my hand and teased inside of her. "How's this?"

"It's a start." She half-closed her eyes and gave a sigh. "I don't want you to ever stop touching me."

I didn't want that either. Ever.

I stroked her clit with a slow, lazy rhythm.

"Be my fake girlfriend."

Savannah arched her hips to meet my finger. "I don't know…"

I kissed her deeply, as I added a second finger, searching out the perfect angle. She'd been wet to begin with from our sex, but now she was getting excited again, her body slick with want. "Be my fake girlfriend, Savannah. Please. Pretty fucking please."

"Mad…" She gripped my waist and gave a soft moan. "Oh, Mad, that feels so…"

I found her spot, the one that always made her suck in a harsh breath before she came. "Be my fake girlfriend," I demanded.

She fell over the edge. "Yes, oh, God, yes." She came with a shudder and closed eyes.

There was nothing hotter than watching Savannah find satisfaction.

"You said yes. I'm holding you to that."

Savannah opened her eyes. "That was a dirty trick." She wetted her bottom lip with her tongue and stared at me through slumberous eyes. "You're a very bad man."

"Only in appearance." I gave her a smile. "I have a heart of fucking gold."

I was joking, but she actually sighed. "Actually. You do." She trailed her fingers over my hip. "Yes, I will do it. I'll come to the shop."

I kissed her forehead. "Thank you."

"It's the least I can do. You're doing a lot for me." She shifted her hand and stroked over my cock. "This alone is worth whatever you want."

My ego swelled about as huge as my cock. "I think I'm blushing."

She laughed. "No, you're not. Now get a new condom. Please."

"Yes, ma'am."

She smacked my arm. "Ew, don't call me ma'am. That makes me feel old."

"Yes, sexy ass. How's that?" I reached behind me for the condom box, grateful for long arms. I tore a packet open.

"We'll work on it." Savannah helped me roll the condom on and then she shifted and got on top.

Now I was the one moaning. "Fuck, Savannah."

She moved her hips, her hands on my chest. Her hair slid over her chest, cheeks flushed with arousal. There was nothing sexier than seeing her ride my cock, taking her pleasure for herself.

"I can't get enough of this cock."

"Take as much as you want."

We were playing a dangerous game and I think we both knew

it. We were having sex every day. Every single day. At some point we needed to talk about what the hell we were actually doing, but for friends with benefits, we'd been benefiting without interruption.

But right then, I didn't care. All I cared about was watching her sweet ass rise and fall onto me, her hand lifting to toss her hair back.

When she came, I was right there with her.

It was amazing.

It was also a problem.

Because I *was* right there with her.

Savannah fell onto my chest with a soft laugh. "That wasn't fake."

I lightly smacked her ass. "Nope. And for the record, I'm not faking a damn thing."

There was so much truth to that, and part of me hoped she heard it.

JUST DROP by the tattoo shop. Maddox said that was all I needed to do. Just walk in, say hi to everyone, walk back out.

Oh, and pretend to be his girlfriend.

I should have hated the idea, but the truth was, I was kind of gleeful at the idea. It was a way to take the closeness he and I shared in my apartment and show it in public. Which made it really stupid. Like playing house. Which we were already doing. What was yet another layer to add to our complicated relationship?

"This might be a bad idea," Felicia said to me as she got comfortable on my apartment floor, rolling a ball to Sully.

She had agreed to watch him for an hour, but she obviously thought this was all bonkers. "Why? He's coming to the engagement party with me as my date."

"Which is also a bad idea. You're blurring lines. You're spending an extraordinary amount of time together as it is. Now you're lying to his co-workers while filming it for television? That seems like an utter disaster."

"I'm in total control of it," I lied. "I'm just saving Maddox from getting fired. This is a huge deal to him. He needs the money to open his own shop. How could I say no to him? He's helped me so much."

My vagina. He'd *really* helped my vagina.

"I'm not going to criticize you or tell you I think you're insane like Isla would but I'm just saying I'm concerned about you getting hurt at the end of all of this."

"And I appreciate that." I did a mirror check by the door. I was wearing a hat and a green sweater with a rust-colored jacket. Black skinny jeans, boots that should make me look taller. I wanted Maddox's friends to think I was put together. I refused to wear yoga pants to a tattoo shop run entirely by a staff minutes out of their teen years. "I know you're worried about me. But…" I turned and looked at her. "I can't stop myself, Felicia. I really can't."

It was painful to admit that. But it was true.

"Oh, dear," she said. "You've fallen for him, haven't you?"

"Sort of. Maybe. I don't know." Which was the truth. "All I know is right now I'm enjoying being with him and if I can help him, I could never tell him no."

"All right, then. Just be careful. I still can't believe you rejected Michael. He seemed so brilliant when I was chatting with him."

"He was very nice. That wasn't the issue. Maybe a different time or a different place, it would have been different." I eyed her. "I think you have a crush on him and I think you should go on that app as yourself, not me, and message him."

That effectively turned the subject from me and Maddox. She instantly started shaking her head. "I can't. No. Absolutely not. That's not me. You know I can dole out advice for days when it comes to everyone else, but I am an utter failure at dating."

"You seemed to do just fine talking to Michael as me."

"That was on my phone, messaging. Totally different."

I rolled my eyes and gave her a smile. "Don't shortchange yourself. Okay, I'm off. I'll be back in a bit, thank you!"

The shop was basically what I had pictured. Cool, artistic, filled with tattooed and pierced people. Jana was behind the front desk and saw me and came running straight up to me. She hugged me before I could even react to the unexpected greeting, as well as the fact that there was a camera crew taking up one whole corner of the shop.

"Hi Savannah," she said, pulling back. "I'm so glad to see you here."

"Oh! Hi. Nice to see you again." The greeting seemed more effusive than necessary given we'd met once for two minutes, but I knew she and Maddox had become good friends. The way he talked about her it was clear she had a big personality, so maybe the hug wasn't unusual. Jana was beautiful. She had high cheekbones, flawless skin, and a mischievous grin that was on full display.

"I have heard everything about you. You're all Maddox talks about."

Really? That was interesting. Or maybe that was part of the non-reality part of the reality show. "We both know Maddox is more the strong but silent type," I said. "I don't see him gushing about me at work."

Jana laughed. "Fair enough. I always tell him he's pragmatic and he hates it. Come on over and meet everyone."

She took me by the hand, which amused me, and basically dragged me around, introducing me to the camera crew. Maddox appeared from a back room and I was suddenly overwhelmed by how incredibly sexy he was. He belonged here, that was obvious. He walked with confidence and it was hard sometimes to remember how young he actually was. He saw me and gave me a smile that made my insides warm.

"Hey," he said. "Thanks for coming by."

Then he kissed me, which I guess I should have seen coming, but hadn't. It was no quick peck. It wasn't "get a room" either, but it was beyond a friendly greeting. My face felt hot when he pulled back.

"Of course," I said. "I'm excited to see where you're working. This is a great shop."

Jana was next to us, bouncing on the balls of her feet. "Do you have any tattoos, Savannah?"

"Me? No."

"Are you afraid of needles?"

I shook my head. "Not really. I just never felt connected enough to anything to ink it on my body permanently."

Jana nodded. "Not a bad philosophy. I have a milk carton inked on my leg. I'm random and impulsive."

"She is," Maddox said. "She falls in and out of love with people, hobbies, and food with amazing speed."

They seemed to know each other really well and I felt just a teeny tiny bit jealous of that. "As long as you don't get hurt, that's probably a great way to live. No regrets."

"Oh, I never regret anything." She gave me a look that seemed searching. "No one wants regrets, right?"

I felt like she was trying to tell me something, but what, I had no idea.

Maddox took my hand and introduced me to Samuel, who was adorable and quite the flirt, then to Stella, who was polite, but slightly bitchy. Travis seemed genuinely curious about me.

"Maddox is a steel trap. He never talks about his personal life. It's cool to meet you."

That seemed more accurate than Jana's claim he talked nonstop about me. Probably true, but slightly disappointing. But why would he talk about me? We weren't really a couple.

Even though his hand in mine felt really, really natural.

Felicia might have been right. This was a stupid, muddy-the-waters thing to do.

"This is a great shop," I told Travis. "What an amazing accomplishment at your age."

He grinned. "Thanks. You can't be afraid to just go for it. What's the worst thing that can happen, right?"

That casual comment gave me goosebumps.

So many thoughts were swirling through my head and I didn't want to acknowledge any of them.

"I want a tattoo," I blurted out.

"What?" Maddox looked at me like I had legitimately shocked him. "Of what?"

I turned to him, conviction growing. "I don't know. Something about the baby. Maybe a heart or his initials? His birthdate?"

Maddox's expression softened. "I think that's an awesome idea." He brushed my hair back off my cheek. "But you should think about it for a few weeks. We can bounce some ideas around."

I nodded. He was right. Sullivan was my family, and had changed my life forever for the better, and I wanted to display that but I didn't want to just pick something randomly to represent what he meant to me.

"Boo," Jana said. "You're a buzzkill, Mad. Savannah, I say go for it right now."

"I think I got swept in the atmosphere," I said. And maybe the cameras. I was used to filming myself, but not having a crew. It was definitely a different vibe.

I pictured my brother's reaction to Maddox kissing me and decided I didn't care.

Maddox was exactly what I needed in my life.

I was introduced to the producer and put in a chair next to Maddox.

"How long have you been seeing each other?" I was asked by Mark, from his position behind the cameraman.

The formality of it was disconcerting but Maddox and I had rehearsed. "Just six weeks. But we've known each other for fifteen years."

Maddox squeezed my knee. I looked over at him. He gave me a smile that was more dirty than loving.

"Did you have feelings for him before?"

I turned back to the camera and the producer. "Uh, sure, friendship. But not romantic."

"I had romantic feelings for her," he said. "She just thought I was annoying."

"That's not true! I never thought you were annoying. I just never… thought about it." I inwardly winced. That sounded horrible.

"Is Maddox romantic?"

That question caught me off guard. "What? What do you mean?" I asked, stalling.

"Does he bring you flowers or write you notes? Take you to rooftop dinners?"

Who went to rooftop dinners? I didn't even think that was a thing. "Not those things in particular, no."

"So he's not romantic?"

"I didn't say that." What the hell? I was being setup and now I was flustered. "I have a baby. We can't go out on glamorous dates right now." That was one hundred percent the truth.

"What made you fall for him now then?"

Oh God. So many things. His smile. His laugh. His kindness. His hard muscles. The way he stared into my eyes when he pushed inside my body.

I cleared my throat. My cheeks felt hot.

"His ink, of course. Who doesn't love a hot guy with some great tats?"

Everyone laughed.

"Nice maneuver," Mark said. "I love it."

I didn't even want to think about what I loved because I was starting to have a sneaking suspicion it was Maddox.

Chapter 12

Maddox opened the door for me at the venue hosting Leah and Grant's engagement party the following Friday night. I barely had time to react to the decor of the room in front of me when Dakota spotted me and came in for a hug.

"Oh my God, you look so hot!" she exclaimed. "Hot mama!"

I laughed. "Thanks." I did actually feel decidedly not mom-ish. I was wearing a deep navy sparkly cocktail dress that was so short I was at risk for flashing if I sat down carelessly. My heels were the highest I'd worn in eighteen months. I'd gotten a blowout and I had hair that was big and bold, sort of a nod to the eighties. It felt fantastic to feel put together and sexy.

Dakota always looked sexy. Always. She had legs that were a thousand miles long and a confident walk. She was wearing a black jumpsuit with a plunging neckline. At six feet tall she could be seen halfway across the lobby. Wherever she went, she turned heads, usually because she chose to wear high heels all the time. She always joked that she was constantly mistaken for a drag queen, but that wasn't going to stop her from wearing heels because drag queens were amazing.

"You look gorgeous too," I told her. "This is Maddox. Maddox, this is Dakota."

"Nice to meet you." He reached out and shook her hand.

It was kind of crazy they hadn't met yet but the last six weeks had just flown by.

Dakota eyed him with naked curiosity. "So this is the manny? It's a *pleasure* to meet you."

I knew what she saw, because I saw it too. Maddox was sexy and dangerous and gorgeous looking all at once. He was wearing a suit, but it didn't disguise all of his tattoos. The ones on his hands and fingers were still visible. The suit also didn't hide the fact that he was ripped either. It only emphasized it. For a guy who had to be one of the sweetest, most solid men I'd ever met, his dark eyes smoldered.

"It's nice to meet you too." He gave me an amused look when Dakota didn't let go of his hand.

"Let go of him," I told her with a laugh.

"Oops. Sorry, not sorry." But given she was Dakota, she just turned and swept her arm across the room. "This is just the lobby and look at this. You're going to die when you see the actual ballroom. I went inside and ran back out because I needed to experience it with someone else. You can't go in alone, trust me on this."

We were at the Chelsea Pier and I had noticed decking that went around the whole perimeter, given a fantastic view of the Hudson river. The Jersey City skyline was twinkling on the opposite bank.

"Leah said the pier location was a nod to Grant having been in the navy," I told Maddox. "I think that's very cool, to make it personal."

"If the pier is about the navy, then the ballroom is about being inside an acid trip," Dakota said. "It's *insane*."

The doors were opened for us by men in tails and Dakota did not lie.

"Holy shit..." was Maddox's opinion.

I was momentarily speechless. It was an explosion of color and ribbons and flowers and... humans dangling from aerial ribbons. It was the circus. It was the Big Top married with Vegas while cheating on Vegas with the Moulin Rouge. Or maybe Versailles. Aerial gymnasts floated above us like glamorous little silver specks, twirling and spinning, while the food stations were elevated train cars.

I grabbed Maddox's arm and bounced up and down a little. "It's the theater! It's the theater meets the circus meets the navy! Look, there's a pinup girl sailor!" I couldn't help myself. I absolutely loved when couples personalized an engagement party and a wedding. Over the top? Extra AF? Bring it on. I loved it.

Besides, not everyone had the kind of budget they did. They had the cash and they'd clearly decided to just throw a wild ride of an engagement party.

"It's something," Maddox said. "I feel inappropriately dressed. Like I should be wearing a top hat and a velvet tuxedo."

Felicia appeared beside us. "Do you get the feeling this is actually a wedding?" she asked.

"Oooh," I said. "Maybe. It does seem like a lot for an engagement party. Now, that would be so romantic. A surprise wedding? I love it."

"Wouldn't Leah tell us?" Dakota asked. "A surprise wedding doesn't seem like her thing. That's more your thing, Savannah."

Admittedly, it was.

Isla, who must have arrived with Felicia grabbed a glass of champagne off of a passing server tray and raised it in front of us. "I don't think it's a wedding. They're doing this to both satisfy and annoy Grant's family. If I had to bet money, I would say they get married solo on a beach or something. This is extravagant because there won't be a wedding reception."

"That might be true." Though the idea disappointed me.

"Isla, you remember Maddox, my friend and nanny extraordinaire." I smiled at him. God, he looked handsome in his suit. It was such a change from his usual black-on-black-with-metal outfit choices.

He *was* an amazing nanny. He was an amazing person. Sully loved him and Maddox's style was easy, playful. Nothing rattled him. Not spit-up. Not full diapers. Not three-in-the-morning crying jags. Some day he was going to make an awesome father.

The knowledge was one that constantly knocked at my thoughts. Maddox probably didn't want to get married and have kids for another decade. He still had the majority of his twenties ahead of him to have fun, establish a business, date around and get married. I was really going to miss him when he left. There would be a lucky woman in his future.

Which made me sick to my stomach every time I considered it.

ISLA GREETED MADDOX, but she also gave me a long, searching look that made my cheeks feel hot. What did she see? Did she know that I was completely full of shit when I said my feelings for Mad were one hundred percent platonic and familial?

They already all knew we were having sex, but I'd thought only Felicia had caught on to how much deeper it was going than that. But given the look on Isla's face, she was onto me as well.

"It's great to see you again," she told Maddox. "I think it's great you'd give up your Friday night to protect Savannah from the evil clutches of a dick she went out with once weeks ago."

I glared at Isla. "Don't be so sarcastic. You sound rude."

"I never turn down an invitation to an open bar," Maddox said, mildly.

"Dude," Dakota said. "Right? Speaking of, I say we head over there and do some shots to kick this party off on the right note."

"Dakota, I can't drink," I reminded her for the hundredth time in the last year plus.

"Oh, fuck, I always forget that. Well, you can go find our table while we do shots."

"You're so good to me," I said to her, rolling my eyes and laughing.

"What? I'm sorry. You know I'm not mom material. I'm not trying to be a jerk."

"I know." I pointed. "Go. Go do a shot. Do one for me. I will find the table."

"I'll go with you," Maddox said.

"No!" Dakota said. "Open bar, remember?"

"I can get something later. My job is to visibly adore Savannah."

Hell, yes.

"Oh, that sounds kinky," Dakota said. "I'm jealous." But then she turned. "See you later!"

"Sorry," Felicia said. "I really want a drink." She gave me a finger wave and followed suit.

"Are you abandoning me for booze too?" I asked Isla.

She nodded. "You don't need me anyway. You have Maddox."

Except I didn't *have* him.

"It's you and me, kid," he said. "Are you hungry? It looks like there's enough food to feed the entire eastern seaboard."

"I'm going to smash on all of it," I said cheerfully. "And not feel remotely guilty. A party like this is all about the food and the DJ."

"Wait until you see my dance moves," Maddox said.

He did a hip swivel that made me laugh. "What was that?"

"The Elvis. I can floss too but I'm saving that for the end of the night."

"Can't wait." I maneuvered around some tables and scanned the first food station. "I am a terrible dancer. Which was why my original career choice when I came to New York was to be an actress. I can't dance and can't sing, so that limited my options considerably."

"I remember you wanted to make it big."

"I was delusional," I said laughing. "I used to tell my father I was an optimist, a dreamer, and he would tell me I needed to get my head out of the clouds. Turns out in that particular instance he was right. I couldn't see that I wasn't good enough to land roles until I had cranky directors tell me no over and over."

"You clearly landed where you're supposed to but don't ever lose that dreamer quality, Savannah. It's what makes you you and it's beautiful."

I was unexpectedly touched. "Thank you."

Maddox lifted up a canape and popped it into his mouth. "Damn, that's good." He grabbed another one and held it to my lips.

Being fed by him seemed incredibly intimate but I didn't back away. I just parted my lips and accepted the bite. I was chewing but I barely tasted the food. In the midst of the glamourous room filled with insane décor and people dressed to the nines, all I could see was Maddox.

Until the lights turned down two seconds later and a carnival caller came over the loud speaker. I turned, dying to see what was going to happen.

"What the hell?" Maddox asked. "Is Leah coming down from the ceiling on a giant swing?"

She was.

"That is amazing," I said. "She's straight-up Moulin Rouge."

The announcer started singing. Maddox's eyebrows shot up. "This is crazy."

It was. Especially since a car pulled up and Grant got out of it. A car. In the ballroom. He stood and waited for her swing to hit the ground, then he took her hand, they got back into the car, and drove it across the length of the ballroom, waving to all the guests.

They parked at the edge of the dance floor and got out.

"What now?" Maddox murmured. "I mean, seriously, where do you go from here?"

"Space?" I suggested. "I love it. I love everything about this."

What they actually did was end up surrounded by all the aerial gymnasts descending down onto the dance floor, swept up onto a platform that had two chairs shaped like circus elephants. "They're sitting on fake elephants," I said. "I mean… wow."

"When you told me Grant was a billionaire I just pictured something more reserved. Like a state dinner or something."

"I wasn't picturing that. I was thinking trendy and fun. But Leah did tell me they had a joke that they wanted a circus wedding. I didn't think she meant it literally but I guess I was wrong."

"Maybe the wedding will be more traditional."

"After seeing this, who knows?" I said.

We all clapped and cheered as Grant and Leah were introduced as the future Mr. and Mrs.

"I'm so happy for them," I said. "They're so adorable."

It made me happy sigh to see them smiling at each other.

Long live love.

THE NIGHT WAS A BLAST. I watched Savannah dancing with her friends and grinned. She was right. She wasn't a very coordinated dancer. She always seemed one split second off the beat. Or maybe it was that next to Dakota no one was going to look like a star. Dakota had every guy in the room vying for her attention on the dance floor.

Every guy except for me.

I only had eyes for Savannah.

As I stood on the edge of the dance floor sipping a bourbon, I watched her laughing, head tipping back. She was definitely the woman who did not need alcohol to have a great time. She was in awe of everything, enthusiastic, and quick to relish other people's happiness.

I was totally fucking in love with her.

I mean, we knew that, right? I just hadn't been able to acknowledge the full truth of it.

One hundred percent, all in, give-me-forever in love with her. That's what I was.

Now I just had to convince her she was in love with me too.

Because I had a sneaking suspicion she was. It was there, in her eyes, when she smiled at me.

During sex, when she broke beneath me, my name on her lips.

When she handed me her son with complete trust.

We hadn't encountered Yates Caldwell, her date from hell, and I was glad. I didn't want to see him and get pissed that he had called her a bitch in a text. He needed his watch to tell him if she got him hot? Fuck off, dude. Such bullshit.

I knew Jana wanted me to punch him in the face, and trust me, I really wanted to, but that was bad form for an engagement party, even one that looked like the inside of a Beatles song circa 1973. The guy was the future groom's cousin. It wouldn't be cool to knock his teeth out, though I had every confidence that I could.

All of a sudden, Savannah stopped dancing and pressed her arms to her chest. She quickly departed the dance floor. When she spotted me she rushed straight over.

"What's wrong?" I asked. She didn't look like she'd turned an ankle or anything.

"My milk," she hissed. "It's all over my dress."

I looked down at her chest. Sure enough, there were two large wet spots on the front of her dress. It wasn't super obvious given that her dress was navy blue, but I could understand why she'd be upset. "Here." I peeled off my jacket and flung it around her shoulders.

She relaxed a little, dropping her arms so she could tug the jacket closed over her chest. "I hope no one saw anything."

"I'm sure they didn't. Come on, let's go outside for a minute. The breeze will help your dress dry." I took her hand and drew her towards the balcony. It wrapped around three sides of the building with a very cool view of the river and the skyline. The area closed to the doors had several people out there, some smoking, some just talking away from the loud music.

It was cold, but not unbearable.

"You're going to freeze without your jacket," Savannah protested as I pulled her around the side of the building.

"I told you, the cold doesn't really bother me. We'll just stay out here for a few minutes." We could hear the music spilling out the open doors. "I'll show you my moves like I promised." I gave her some more hip thrusts to the beat.

She laughed, putting her arms through the sleeves of my suit jacket. "You're very proud of those moves."

"Did I tell you I know how to ballroom dance? I know the waltz in particular." I did a few steps like I had a partner.

"What? When did you learn to ballroom dance?"

"When I was ten. It was part of my mom's plan for her wedding with Mike. She and I did a choreographed dance, then at the end Mike cut in and shook my hand. Needless to say, everyone loved it. People were crying." I leaned against the railing to look at her. "I just thought it was cool there was a chocolate fountain. At the end of the night Mike let me stick my face in it."

"And now you can dance?" Savannah asked, coming over and leaning on the railing next to me. She was facing the river.

"That I can."

And as luck would have it (though Jana might call it fate), the music turned from a pounding dance song to something slow and sensual. I held my hand out. "Come here, Savannah."

For a second, I thought she was going to refuse. But then she just took my hand and let me pull her against me.

"I don't know how to waltz," she said.

"Just follow me." I took her hand, and put my hand firmly on the small of her back. Then I spun her around.

"Oh!" she said, spinning on her heels, her hair flying out around her. "I wasn't expecting that."

"Were you expecting this?" I asked, pulling her tight against my body as I just swayed gently with her.

We moved together, easily, and she smiled. "It's really beautiful out here."

"You're really beautiful." I bent down and kissed her with everything I felt inside of me. All my love and passion for her.

The wind blew around us and the lights of the city reflected off the water and it was perfect. She was perfect.

Savannah kissed me back until we heard someone say "Oh, whoops!"

She pulled back and gave me an amused look. "I think we just got caught," she said in a stage whisper.

I glanced to my left. It was four people in their fifties or sixties passing a shared cigarette. Or possibly a blunt. "We most definitely did."

"Can we go home?" she asked.

Home. Yeah. That would be my heart just about busting out of my chest.

"We can do whatever you want, Savannah. Anything."

She stared up at me, her eyes bright. "Then take me home, Maddox."

Chapter 13

WHEN WE GOT BACK to the apartment, Savannah went to check on the baby while I walked the babysitter downstairs to make sure she got in a cab safely. It all felt very much like we were a couple, living together, raising a baby.

In love.

I returned to the apartment after saying goodnight to Ida right as Savannah emerged from the bedroom wearing sweatpants and a sweatshirt. Both were large and loose enough to fit on an NFL player. She was drowning in them and I was disappointed. I preferred the sexy dress. I'd been anticipating sliding a hand up that short skirt.

The outfit might be a setback but I wasn't going down without a fight. She was getting her water bottle out of the refrigerator and I leaned against the counter next to her, studying her, wanting to know where her head was at. On the deck, there had been a moment where I'd thought she was right there, with me. Falling in love.

"What's the most romantic thing I could do right now?" I asked her. "What would be the perfect rom-com ending to a great night?"

Her nose wrinkled. "What? What are you talking about?"

"How would this end in the movies?" I reached out and took

her free hand and laced my fingers through hers. I kissed her knuckles one by one.

"I… I don't know."

"No? Not a single idea?"

Savannah set her water down and shook her head. "We order a pizza?"

I gave her a look. "Really? That's the best you've got? I can see I'm going to have to take charge of this." I turned and pried open the kitchen window. "We're going to sit on the fire escape and look at the stars."

Her jaw dropped. "Are you serious? Is that even safe?"

"It's a fire escape. It's meant to be for you to escape fire. Safely. Of course it's safe." I stuck my head out and assessed it. The first time I'd been in the kitchen I'd thought if I lived here in the summer I'd be sitting out there all the time. "Are you telling me you've never been out here?"

"No! I'm a mother."

"I didn't say bring the kid out here. But before he was born or when he's in bed you've never sat out here and looked around at the neighborhood? The sky?"

"No. It never even occurred to me."

"And you call yourself the rom-com queen." I scoffed. "Wasted opportunity."

She eyed the window. "What if we get locked out?"

"Take your keys if somehow mysteriously the window both closes and locks itself on the inside without human interference."

Savannah gave me a frown.

I laughed. "What?" I stuck my head out. "This is amazing. Here, I'll test it first." I crawled out and jumped up and down on it a few times.

She gave a sound of distress but the platform didn't even move. "It's very solid," I told her. "I promise."

I came back in and went to the living room to grab the blanket I used to sleep. I yanked off my tie and tossed it on the couch. Then I got a beer for myself from the fridge. "Grab your keys."

If I went out, I figured she'd follow me. I was right. She did go and get her house keys, but then she held on to the window frame and crawled through the opening. She kept holding it as she stood and got her bearings.

"This is kind of cool, I'm not going to lie." Still clinging to the building, she slid down onto the blanket I had spread out for us to sit on. "Put these in your pocket," she said, handing me the keys.

I did as I was told. Then we settled in next to each other, leaning against the open window frame, my arm around her. She leaned on me and pulled the blanket over both of us. "This is definitely a different perspective on the neighborhood. It's chilly though."

"It is November," I said. "But five minutes. That's all I ask. Look at the sky. Then look at me. Because I have something I need to tell you."

SOMETHING about the tone in Maddox's voice had me turning quickly toward him, my heart racing. "What?"

But he shook his head. "Look at the sky first, Savannah."

I swallowed my need to ask him again and did as he asked. I was amazed at how bright it was despite it being midnight. Light pollution made the sky look like it was only a step or two past dusk tonight. The air was cool and crisp and there really weren't any visible stars. But the sky was a beautiful canopy arching over the tops of the buildings. All of the adjacent apartments were brick with the same lattice work of fire escapes. Lights dotted the windows of various apartments and yet it was surprisingly quiet. It felt like we were alone in the density of Brooklyn.

Leaning against Maddox's strong shoulder I felt overwhelmed by a variety of emotions. I was falling in love with Maddox and that felt both wonderful and wrong. I also felt super grateful for his friendship and companionship. "Thank you," I murmured, not looking at him. "For everything. For being here for me."

He squeezed me closer to his side. "You don't need to thank me. I don't think you understand, Savannah."

His hand gently took my chin and he turned my head. "What

I need to tell you is that I'm in love with you. Not as a little brother or a friend but as a man. The way a man loves a woman he wants to spend forever with."

Each word he spoke sent me further into shock and awe. "Maddox…" I didn't know what to say. My head was screaming at me to protest, to tell him that was insane, he was too young, and we'd only been in each other's lives again for less than two months.

What I actually said was, "I love you, too."

It flew out of my mouth without thought or warning or anything other than my heart speaking for me.

His eyes darkened and his nostrils flared.

I expected him to say something else, but he didn't. He just bent down and took my mouth in a passionate, deep, gorgeous kiss. Our fingers were still laced together and I gave myself over to the moment, to him. There was only me, him, the crisp night air swirling around us and a connection so strong it felt like the iron of the fire escape beneath us.

His free hand started to roam over my body, under the bulkiness of the blanket and my sweats. When he made little circles over my clit, I broke off the kiss, feeling like I couldn't breathe. I gave a little gasp of pleasure, letting my head fall back so I could fully enjoy the sensations he was creating in me.

I found his cock and massaged over the front of his pants, no particular goal in mind, just wanting to feel him.

Maddox definitely had a goal. He went deep and found the perfect angle. I came silently, eyes drifting shut briefly. When the last wave of pleasure settled, I gave a little laugh.

"Oh my God, that was so very high school of me," I breathed. "I just let my brother's best friend finger bang me under a blanket on a fire escape after a party."

Maddox gave a low laugh. "Two major differences though. You would have never let me touch you in high school and if you had, I would have had no clue what to actually do."

That was not an issue now. "Then you've learned a lot in a few short years."

"I should hope so."

"Are we crazy?" I asked, even as I was cozy and content from the orgasm he'd given me. "What are we even doing?" I wasn't sure what it even meant to be in love, or if I was. I knew I loved Maddox, but was that the same thing?

"Don't complicate things. Let's just enjoy each other." He held his hands up like they were forming a box. He raised them toward the sky. "I want to capture this moment. Remember it forever." He turned so his hands were framing my face. "Not that I could ever forget this. You look beautiful. Your eyes are telling me you love me and I've never seen anything so amazing."

I swallowed hard, overwhelmed with the enormity of what I was saying, what we were doing. "I do love you."

He lowered his hands and gave me a slow, wicked smile. "Come inside and show me."

That made me laugh. "Your sex drive is ridiculous."

"You're welcome." He tossed the blanket off of us. "You go in first. I've got your back."

He didn't mean anything by it, I didn't think. But I crawled up onto the window sill and looked back at him. He did. He had my back. I shivered and it wasn't from the cold.

When we got inside, the apartment was brisk from the window being open, but I barely noticed. Maddox unbuttoned his shirt as he walked, peeling it off by the time he reached the couch. I did the same. He took his pants off and sat down, hands resting on his knees after he rolled on a condom.

"Come here," he demanded.

I moved in front of him and he yanked my sweatpants down and lifted me with one hand onto him.

We were deep kisses and hot thrusts. Urgent grappling and hot whispers of love and desire. I rode him until I forgot myself, until I felt the prick of tears at the back of my eyes for no reason. Everything felt hushed and intimate and important.

His hands were on my waist and when I would have shifted, going on my back for him to take over, he held me in place. "No. Don't stop."

So I didn't. I rolled my hips and took him deep inside me, hands on his shoulders, eyes locked together. I wanted to look away. It scared me, the intensity of what I was seeing, feeling, but I couldn't break that gaze. I exploded on him with a cry, and dropped my head on his shoulder.

He took over the rhythm and pounded into me, while I clung to him, eyes damp, wishing I had any sense of self-preservation. Knowing I didn't.

When he came, we sat for seconds that turned to minutes, neither speaking. Neither moving. I was amazed and blown away and terrified all at once.

Finally, he set me off of him.

"Come to bed," I told him, pushing my hair back form my damp forehead.

"What do you mean?"

"I want you to share the bed with me tonight. I can't have you out here on the couch while I'm in there." It just seemed wrong. I wanted him next to me. All hard muscles and warm skin. I wanted his reassurance that this was a good thing, and not the dumbest thing I'd ever done.

"I would like that," he said. He gave me a small smile. "Do you want to be big spoon or little spoon?"

"Little."

"Good. I want to hold you."

The tears burned again and this time I couldn't blink them away.

"Are you crying?" Maddox asked me, reaching for my hand. "What's wrong?" he asked softly. "Talk to me."

But I just shook my head emphatically. I didn't even understand why I was crying. I was happy and scared all at once.

I picked the wrong men.

And they always left me.

I didn't want him to leave me.

"I'm fine," I managed. "Just come to bed." I didn't even wait for him. I left my clothes and my phone in the living room and went into my room. I took the far side so he wouldn't have to walk around the bed and make any more noise than was necessary.

A minute later he came in but I didn't turn to look. I was facing the window, concentrating on the thin ribbons of light from the streetlight coming through the slats. The mattress creaked when his weight eased onto it. I closed my eyes, feeling vulnerable.

To my relief, he didn't speak. He just shifted behind me, his large hand resting on my bare hip. He kissed the back of my head.

My heart rate felt too fast. I took a few deep breaths, and by the time I had, Maddox was asleep, his breathing slow and regular.

A million thoughts were running through my head. I wanted to just enjoy Maddox and our time together. But I didn't trust myself to know what was best for me and that scared the absolute shit out of me.

Sully started to fuss and Maddox jerked awake but just briefly.

Hoping the baby would fall back asleep I stayed still. But his cry wound up and became more urgent, so I got up and brought him to bed. I sat up and let him latch on. Despite the noise, Maddox had fallen back asleep and I stared at his dark hair, his tattooed arms.

Then I looked at my son.

I was either making the best decision or the worst mistake of my life.

In a way, it felt like both.

Chapter 14

MADDOX HAD LEFT on the bus for Stroudsburg and I was freaking out. I called Isla. "Are you hungover?" I asked as a greeting.

"What? No. I didn't actually drink that much last night. Why?"

"I don't want you crankier than you normally are when I tell you something."

She sighed. "Please don't tell me you're pregnant."

"What?" The thought hadn't actually occurred to me. We'd been cautious but it wasn't impossible. Great. Now I had a whole new fear. "No. I'm not pregnant. Not that I know of." I was sitting on the couch feeding Sully. "Maddox told me he loves me and I said it back."

"Oh, Jesus. Well, okay, so… now what?"

"I don't know, that's the problem. But I do know I can't go out on a date with the guy you picked out for me."

"That's good to hear because I never actually did that."

That caught me off guard. "What? Why not? I thought you said you know some guy from work."

"To be honest, I thought you would wind up in a relationship with the very first date. That's how you're built."

"I don't even know what to say to that."

"Because it's true."

"I don't know what's true anymore." I propped my phone on

my shoulder and switched Sully from one breast to the other. Motherhood had taught me to be a great multitasker. Which proved to be even more necessary when my door buzzed. "Hang on, someone is buzzing my door. It's probably meant for one of my neighbors."

We had a camera feature and an app that allowed us to see who was at the door and to unlock it for them if they were legit. When I saw who was at the door, I dropped the phone. I scrambled to pick it back up and stared at the screen. Yep. It was Adam. Sully's father.

I put the phone back to my ear. "Isla, I have to go."

"Why? What's wrong?"

She could obviously hear the panic in my voice.

"Adam is at my door."

"Asshole Adam?"

"Yes." I pulled Sully off my breast, even though he mildly complained. I raised him to my shoulder, feeling sick to my stomach.

"Savannah, don't answer the door. Have Maddox talk to him. I'm serious. That guy is a loose cannon."

I hesitated. I wanted to know what the hell he wanted but she was right. "Maddox isn't here."

"Then don't answer the door. He shouldn't just show up on your doorstep. That's not cool."

I took a deep breath. She was right. The buzzer went off again. "Let me call you back. I promise I won't let him in."

"Savannah, don't—"

I ended the call and used the intercom feature on the app. "What are you doing here, Adam?"

"I have papers for you to sign. Let me in, Savannah."

I hated confrontation and I hated being tough. It wasn't in my nature. "I'm sorry, I can't do that. Just leave whatever it is at my door. I'll buzz you in."

Hitting the button, I adjusted my bra and shirt and held Sully tightly to me. I made sure my door was locked as I heard him bounding up the flight of stairs.

The knock made me jump.

"Savannah, open the door. I just want to talk to you."

He didn't sound angry, but I was still unnerved. "I don't think that's a good idea."

Sully was starting to fuss, having been cut short from his breakfast.

"Is that my son?" he asked. The knocking came again, and it was more like pounding this time. "Savannah. Open the fucking door. Please."

Part of me wished Maddox was there. The other part of me was glad he wasn't. I didn't need a confrontation between the two of them. Besides, I wanted to be the one to handle the situation. Isla was calling me but I didn't answer. I wasn't sure what was the right thing to do, but I had to do something. Process of elimination led me to the conclusion my best option was to make plans to talk to him on my terms.

"Adam, if you want, I can meet you at the coffee shop in a few hours, but I can't open this door." There was no way in hell I was jeopardizing Sully's safety. Not happening. He could bang on that door all damn day. "Now you should leave before the neighbors call the cops on you. I'll text you a time." After I found a sitter for the baby.

He swore but he did say, "Fine. I'll see you later, then."

"Yes." I wanted to walk a fine line between being polite so he didn't flip out and not being nicer than he deserved. The sound of his voice, which I had once thought was so charming, made my stomach turn.

I waited until it sounded like he'd gone down the stairs before going to the door and looking out the peephole. The hallway appeared to be empty. I sagged against the metal door. I checked the camera downstairs and saw him leave.

Then I called Isla back as I opened the door to retrieve whatever he'd left. I juggled Sully on my hip.

"What the hell happened?"

"He said he had paperwork to give me. I didn't let him in. It's an envelope, kind of thick, but nothing sketchy."

"Open it."

I shut and locked the door and put Sully down on his mat with a shape-sorter toy.

It took me a second to pull out the paperwork and scan through it. "It's some kind of one-time payout to me, then his request to terminate parental rights."

"Wow. How do you feel about that?"

Everything. Nothing. "I honestly don't know. I told him I'd meet him in a couple of hours. Can you watch Sully for me? Maddox is at his parents' in Stroudsburg for the day."

"I don't understand why you need to meet him. Just sign the papers and be done with him. I mean he's basically buying your silence. Giving you money so you'll never bother him again."

"I know." I swallowed and looked at my son. "I don't know if that's better or worse than the guy who is in and out of a child's life."

"I don't either." She sighed. "Fine. I can watch Sully but only for an hour. I have to be at the restaurant at three today and you know what Saturday is like this time of year. I can't be late."

"I promise."

"Please be careful. Meet him in public and maybe take some pepper spray with you."

That made me roll my eyes. "He's not going to attack me." I didn't think. "He didn't even sound angry."

Though he did refer to Sullivan as his son and that worried me. I hadn't even realized he knew whether I'd had a boy or girl.

"I'll see you in half an hour, give or take forty minutes depending on how the train is running."

"Thanks, you're the best."

"I would never let anything happen to you, you know that right?" she said. "You're my best friend and I'm a bulldog to your Pomeranian."

I did. My heart warmed. "I know. Though I've always pictured myself more as an Irish setter. Glamorous, with great hair."

She laughed. "How do you picture me?"

"Bulldog sounds right," I joked.

"Bitch."

"I love you, Isla."
"Whatever."

LILLIAN WAS HANGING on my back, her favorite position, while I popped sugared walnuts into my mouth. Occasionally I would drop down so that Lil almost fell and she would squeal with laughter. I'd missed my family and I was glad to be home, even though the timing sucked. I had wanted nothing more than to spend the entire day loving on Savannah.

I love you, too.

Those words had come out of her mouth. Savannah Prescott had said she loved me and the whole world was bright and shiny and new and fucking perfect.

I'd never been happier and nothing could wreck my mood.

"Lillian, give me a minute with your brother," my mother said, coming over to the buffet table where I was hunkered down.

"I don't want to leave," Lillian complained.

"Go," my mother said in that voice that meant business. She pointed to the other side of the room.

Lillian jumped down off of me and ran off. I had the distinct impression I was in trouble. Which shouldn't scare me at my age but did make me uneasy. I loved my mother too much to not care if she was pissed at me.

"Are you enjoying your birthday?" I asked. "You look great, by the way."

She crossed her arms and gave me a suspicious look. She had her hair curled and full makeup on. Despite it being lunchtime she was wearing super tight jeans and boots that went over her knees. Her nails were painted black and her sweater did a plunge that I'm sure Mike appreciated but I could do without. But that was my mother.

"Don't be sarcastic," she said. "I know you don't like the way I dress."

"I was not being sarcastic. I really mean you look great. How you dress is your business," I said, sincerely. "It's not that I don't like it. I just never enjoyed being out in public with you when I was nineteen and having people think we were a couple." Most awkward thing ever.

She laughed. "Trust me, I didn't enjoy that either. The older we both get the odder our age difference seems. When I was eighteen and you were three, it all seemed natural and normal. But now you're a grown man and I'm not even forty. It's bizarre."

"Especially given how mature I am," I joked, reaching for another nut. "These things are like candy, by the way."

"Don't talk about nuts. I'm mad at you," she said.

There it was. I had known she was giving off a vibe. "What did I do?"

"You used to tell me things, Weirdo." Her expression was wounded.

I was used to the nickname. She'd been calling me that as long as I could remember, but in recent years she only used it when she was upset or angry. "I tell you things."

"Then why haven't you told me about *her*."

Alarm bells went off. Who knew about Savannah? The show hadn't aired yet and there weren't even clips online yet. Had someone put something on social media? That seemed farfetched.

"About who?" I asked, proceeding with caution.

"Whoever it is that you're in love with, because it's obvious to me, your mother, that you're in love. It's written all over your face."

The problem was I didn't think I could lie to my mother. I could evade, be vague, but I didn't think I could flat-out lie.

"I can't talk about it yet because it just happened," I said. "I don't want to get ahead of myself. But yes, I am in love."

She studied me. "Is it a girl at work?"

I didn't react.

"Someone you met online?"

I just stared at her.

"Is it Savannah?"

I didn't react at all.

Or so I thought.

But her eyes widened. "Holy shit, it's Savannah." She darted her gaze around the room full of people and lowered her voice to a conspiratorial whisper. "Are you sleeping with her?"

"Mom…" I rubbed my jaw.

"Oh my God, you are. You're nailing Savannah, holy shit. I knew a guy and a girl couldn't live together without getting naked. Didn't I tell you that?"

"You literally never told me that. Ever." My mother looked downright gleeful.

"Well, it's true," she said.

"I don't want to talk about anything right now. I don't know if she would want people to know."

She started smiling. She tried to stop herself, pursing her lips, but she couldn't restrain her grin. "Look at you, getting the older woman. I'm impressed."

"Stop. I'm serious." The whole conversation was making me uncomfortable.

"You're dating an older woman?" Mike asked as he came over to snag a jalapeño popper off the table. "Way to go, kid."

"We're not supposed to know," my mother said. "So don't tease him."

I rolled my eyes.

"It's Savannah Prescott," she blurted out.

"Mom!" I gave her an exasperated look.

"What? I don't keep secrets from my husband."

"That is the biggest load of bullshit I've ever heard," Mike said. "But nice attempt at a cover-up." He eyed me. "Is it true?"

"Yes, it's true. But I don't have her permission to be telling all of Stroudsburg, so everyone just keep it on the DL. It's not a secret, exactly, just not something we all need to be talking about or spreading around. Steve doesn't even know and he's in the next freaking room." My best friend had come over to say happy birthday to my mother and hang out with me for a couple hours.

"Lock her in, kid. Otherwise your mother can't be trusted."

She smacked his arm. "Way to have my back, asshole."

Mike kissed her cheek and smacked her butt loudly. "I have your back."

"Gross," was Bianca's opinion as she appeared out of nowhere. "I probably need therapy. You guys are disgusting."

"I agree," I told her. "It's a miracle we're not all fucked up."

"Maddox, don't swear in front of your sister. That is what is fucked up."

And she didn't even see the irony of her words.

"Do you have a problem with me dating someone older?" I asked, because weird or not, my family was important to me.

"No, of course not. I like Savannah. She was always a nice girl."

"You're dating Savannah?" Bianca asked, chomping on a carrot from the vegetable tray.

"Does she love you?" my mother demanded.

"Does who love him?" Steve asked, coming into the room. He stole a carrot out of Bianca's hand and popped it in his mouth.

"Hey!" she said, punching him in the arm.

Great. This was getting dicey. "Mom, when are we getting the cake? I've been off sugar and it looks amazing to me."

"Cake, cake, cake!" Bianca said, fist-pumping.

"I'm not ready for the cake, you heathens."

"Who is in love?" Steve asked, grabbing another beer out of the cooler on the floor. "What did I miss?"

"I'm in love with cake," I said.

My mother just turned and walked away. She clearly didn't trust herself not to say something. I breathed a sigh of relief. Close call. I didn't want to tell Steve until Savannah gave me the green light and I didn't want to tell him in front of my family. I wanted a man-to-man talk. In a public place. Like a bar, where he had a beer.

"You need a life if you're in love with baked goods." But he gave me a look that indicated he knew full well we weren't talking about cake.

My phone chimed in my pocket and I pulled it out. I thought maybe it would be a text from Savannah. Or I was hoping it would be a text from Savannah.

It was actually a message from her friend Isla.

Can you call me? Baby daddy showed up and Savannah is meeting him. I'm worried about it.

That made me frown. "Hey, I have to make a call," I said to the room at large.

I walked into the dining room no one ever used and called her. "Hey, I got your message. What does he want?" I wasn't sure how I was going to feel if he wanted partial custody of Sully. I felt very attached to that little guy.

"He has paperwork he wants her to sign that terminates his parental rights. I don't really understand why he wants to meet her in person to do that. Maybe to try to explain away how much of a prick he is." Isla sounded bitter.

I agreed with her assessment of a man who wouldn't even attempt to see his child at any point. "I don't understand that either. Where is she meeting him? The lawyer's office?" That wouldn't be dangerous in any way.

"The coffee shop. I'm watching Sully."

"Why are you worried? She has told me nothing about him or their relationship." Which was disconcerting now that I thought about it. We were spending a lot of time together. Why hadn't she confided in me what was up with her ex?

"I guess he was fine until the pregnancy. He lost his shit and punched a hole in the wall when she told him. As far as I know, she hasn't seen him since that day."

That did not make me happy. I felt my fists clench. Of all fucking days for me to be gone. It also really bothered me she hadn't shared any of that with me. "Has she been in touch with you since she left? What time is she meeting him?"

"I haven't heard from her but she really just left."

"Keep me posted. Thanks for letting me know. I hate that I'm not there."

There was a pause, then Isla spoke again in a low voice. "I hope you're serious about her, Maddox."

That made me feel like Savannah had told at least Isla about us. "I've never been more serious about anything," I said honestly. "I'm not some fuck boy."

Unfortunately, Steve walked into the room right as I said that.

"Good," Isla said. "I'll call you back."

"Bye." I looked at Steve. "What?"

"I'm taking off. I wanted to say goodbye. So you're a fuck boy? Was that your girl dumping you?"

"Suck my dick."

"Sounds like more than she's doing."

I bit my tongue. He did not want to know where his sister's mouth had been. "Where are you going?"

"I'm hanging out with Kelsey. College football corn hole tournament thing."

Interesting. "You like this girl?"

He shrugged. "She's fun. Don't make more out of it than it is."

I held my hands up. "Calm down. Just curious."

Steve gave me a look as we walked through to the front doorway. "Why haven't you mentioned a girl to me?"

"Because you're not going to like it." I wasn't going to bullshit my best friend.

He swore. "Oh my God, it's my sister, isn't it?"

I didn't confirm or deny. I just kept my mouth shut.

"What the fuck is wrong with you? She's all vulnerable and shit and there you are with your dick?" He looked seriously pissed. "She's exhausted. She's lonely. She hasn't been dating. It's the worst time ever for you to be hooking up with her. Aside from the fact that the very thought makes me want to throw up, it pisses me off you had some fucking agenda. You didn't go to help her, you went to bone her." He pointed a finger at me. "That makes you a selfish prick."

I was shocked by his reaction. "Steve, it's not that. I love Savannah. I've always cared about her. I didn't have some agenda. It just happened." Though that wasn't entirely true, was it? I'd had a plan all along. Aim for a relationship, settle for sex. That had been my plan and he was right—it had been selfish.

"Whatever, Maddox." He shook his head. "This isn't high school. You can't just score the fantasy girl with no thought to the consequences."

I got angry and defensive. "I want to be with her. I know that. If those are the consequences, I'm fucking thrilled with them."

"I don't want to talk about this right now. I'm too pissed. I want to talk to my sister and hear her take on what is happening." He stared at me, his nostrils flaring. "God, fuck you. Just seriously. Fuck you."

He yanked the door open and left, slamming it behind him.

I stared at the door, gut churning. That was worse than I had expected.

"He found out, huh?" Mike asked, wandering down the hallway barefoot, sipping a beer. "Don't worry, he'll come around."

"I think I messed up," I said. "I shouldn't have let him find out until after Savannah said it was cool. And I think he's right—I've been selfish. I was looking at my relationship with Savannah from my point of view. Not hers. I guess I've been thinking I'm a decent catch and hell, maybe I'm not. Maybe I don't have what she needs."

His eyebrows shot up. It was funny. People always thought Mike was my biological father. It was the dark hair, even though his was turning gray now, and the tattoos. We dressed similarly too. He felt like a father to me and I trusted his opinion and advice.

"You are a decent catch. I would argue a great catch. You're honest, loyal, a hard worker, financially stable. You're not ugly and unless you have a secret pencil dick, what is there to complain about?"

Despite my turmoil, that made me laugh. "No pencil dick. I don't know. Maybe she wants something different. Plus it's just Steve said I had an agenda and I guess I did and now that doesn't feel fair to Savannah."

"Son, everyone has an agenda when they're interacting with the opposite sex. Or maybe a goal is a better way to put it. Whether it's an ego boost, or sex, or a relationship. Everyone has a want, a desire, a plan."

I couldn't really argue with that. "True. But I sort of talked about the plan to be with her on the show."

"On the reality show?" he asked, clearly surprised. "Talked about the plan how?"

"Like setups for romantic moments."

For a second Mike just stared at me. Then he said, "Well, that was just stupid. Why would you talk about Savannah on a damn TV show?"

"They wanted me to be more interesting."

"More dumb."

That made me feel like a total ass. "Maybe."

"All I can say is better come clean sooner than later because the longer it goes on, the less likely she is to forgive you."

"I will." I pictured Savannah the night before, tears in her eyes, saying she loved me.

I'd taken them as happy tears, but suddenly I was more than a little concerned this might not go my way.

Plus, she was meeting with Sully's biological father. What if she felt renewed attraction to him?

"I feel like I have to go back to Brooklyn on the next bus."

"Your mother will kill you if you leave her party this soon. Three more hours won't change a damn thing. Just relax."

I wanted to believe he was right.

Checking my phone, I had no texts.

Shoving it back into my pocket, I decided he was right. I went with Mike to talk my mother into cutting her cake.

Chapter 15

SITTING across the table from Adam, who I'd convinced myself I was in love with eighteen months ago, was a bizarre experience. He looked the same. Blond, clean-cut, well-dressed in expensive clothing. He had a charming smile but it wasn't on display right now. He was fiddling with a napkin and sitting way back in his chair, an espresso on the table in front of him.

"You look good," he said. It sounded genuine enough but not like he was longing for me or filled with regrets or anything. "How are you?"

"I'm good," I said, and it was the truth. "Work is letting me work from home, which makes it so much easier." I sipped my latte. "I'm happy to sign the papers, Adam. I don't even find the money necessary. This was never about money."

"I know. I know that about you. By now you could have had me in court to pay child support." He cleared his throat. "I know this doesn't make me look that great, but I don't want this hanging over my head for the next two decades. I just wanted to offer you something but leave everything then up to you."

Basically, he wanted to buy me off. If I signed, I couldn't legally contact him for any financial assistance at any point. "What if I died next year?" I asked.

The question momentarily took him aback, but then he said,

"I'm sure your parents would do an excellent job of raising him. They did with you."

My throat tightened. He really didn't care. He wanted no involvement. None. He had a child and he didn't care, even if something happened to me and Sully was alone. He just wanted to make sure it wouldn't "hang over his head." I felt like the biggest idiot on the planet for falling for a man of his caliber. How could I think he was a good man? I felt gullible as hell and angry with myself. Yes, I was furious with him because he had portrayed himself differently and for being unconcerned about his son but at the same time I was berating myself.

"What if someone wants to adopt him in the future?"

"The document I gave you means I would have no say over that. I'm out. You can legally do whatever you want." He gave me a long look. "I know you already have some guy living with you. Covered in tattoos."

I was taken aback. "Are you spying on me? He's my brother's best friend and he needed a place to stay. He helps me with Sully in return for a couch to sleep on." Or at least, until the night before. "It's not easy to be a working single mom," I added, because he had a lot of freaking nerve.

"Yes, I had someone watching you for a couple of weeks. I wanted to know why you weren't suing me for child support."

"How about I'm independent? And I just didn't want to deal with you."

"Fair enough. For the record, I don't care who the guy is. But I figured he was helping you financially."

"No, he isn't. It's emotional and practical support. The things that really matter." I was still hung up on Adam saying he didn't care who the guy was. It was like another kick in the gut. He didn't care who was spending time with his son. I couldn't wrap my head around that.

When he didn't say anything in response to that, I said, "I'll have a lawyer look at the papers. If everything is fine, I'll sign them as soon as possible. Please don't show up at my apartment again. And don't have anyone creeping on me. It's violating."

He nodded. "I am sorry that I couldn't give you the fairy tale you wanted. You wanted the whole fantasy relationship and I wanted reality."

Somehow, he managed to turn his apology into an insult. He made me sound like some middle school girl.

"I'm not sorry. We clearly don't belong together. But I got my son, so I have no regrets. *My* son."

I thought we had achieved a decent place of understanding until he stood up and slid his arms into his sleeves. "Sign the papers, Savannah, or you will have regrets."

Ew. Dick alert. I made a sound of exasperation. "Don't threaten me, Adam."

He just waved over his shoulder as he left.

"I HAVE the worst taste in men," I told Isla when I got back to my apartment. I took Sully from her and smothered his chubby little cheeks in kisses. I needed to just hold him and convince myself he was safe from the evil clutches of his soulless father.

"We've established this, many times."

"I asked him what would happen if I died and he said he was sure my parents would do a great job raising him. He wants nothing to do with Sully. How could someone feel that way?" I hugged Sully so hard he made a sound of protest.

"A selfish asshole," she said. "Just be glad he showed who he really is sooner than later."

"Thanks for watching him."

"No problem. Um, I have to confess I messaged Maddox and told him you were with Adam."

That startled me. "What? Why?"

"Because I was worried."

"He's in Pennsylvania. What's he supposed to do from there?"

It was unlike Isla and she actually looked sheepish. "In hindsight, I'm not really sure. I just got freaked out."

I was touched. "You love me, Isla Alexander. Just admit it."

She rolled her eyes. "Yes, I do, you trusting-as-fuck Pollyanna.

That's why I was worried. Now tell me what is going on with you and Maddox."

I felt the need to evade that question. "You know exactly what's going on. We're having sex. Very amazing sex." I didn't know why, but I couldn't admit that I had stronger feelings for him. Much stronger feelings. Actually, I did know why. I didn't want to listen to her telling me all the reasons that was crazy.

"When does he get back?"

"Tomorrow."

For a minute, I thought she was going to say something but she just nodded. "Cool. Okay, I have to run. Call me if you need anything."

"I will. Thank you, you're a life saver."

"You're naming the next kid after me."

I laughed. "Of course."

After she left, yelling at me to dead bolt the door behind her, I checked my phone, thinking I would have a text from Maddox. Instead I had a text from my brother.

CALL ME.

That was aggressive. It worried me. Steven wasn't prone to dramatics.

"Hey, how are you? Is everything okay?"

"How long have you been fucking Maddox?"

Oh, shit. "What?" I asked to buy time, my voice rising two octaves. I was so busted. "What do you mean?" As if there was any other meaning for that.

"Don't even try to deny it. He already admitted it and he may be an asshole who banged my sister but he's not a liar."

I was offended. "Don't be crude."

Steven snorted. "Oh, okay. Sorry, how long has Maddox been *making love* to you?" His voice was mocking and dickish.

That really annoyed me. "None of your business. Why do you have such an attitude right now? I'm allowed to have a personal life."

"I don't disagree with that. But you're a single mom for a reason. You get swept up in romance, in the idea of a future."

That actually stung. A lot. So much so that I couldn't think of a single thing to say.

Which didn't matter, because he wasn't done telling me his opinion of my dating life. "Maddox has had a crush on you since ninth grade. The kind of crush that involves hand lotion and a catch-all sock."

"What does that mean?" I asked. A sock?

"He was jerking off to thoughts of you, that's what it means."

Oh, geez. I got the sock reference then. Yuck. "So what? That was ten years ago."

"This was his plan. To finally get in your pants. The nerd gets the hot girl."

"I think you're exaggerating. Maddox is no nerd these days and frankly right now, I'm not the hot girl. I wear a lot of sweat-pants." I was longing for them as we spoke. I'd put on a cute dress for my meet-up with Adam.

"He's taking advantage of you being lonely and vulnerable."

I took a deep breath. "Steven. I appreciate you caring about me. But I am not some desperate chick who falls on the first guy who shows her interest."

Even as I spoke the words out loud, I wondered if that was a total lie.

I did do that.

Holy shit.

Wait. No, I didn't. Maybe in the past I'd been a little too eager, but look at how I had turned down Yates Caldwell, the DJ whose name I couldn't remember, and Michael the widower. I was a strong and independent woman unwilling to settle.

Or was that because I'd already gotten emotionally attached to Maddox?

That was an uncomfortable thought.

Because yes, I was emotionally attached to Maddox.

"How did you find out about us?"

"He was on the phone talking to someone about it. I heard him."

That bothered me. "Talking to who?"

"I don't know. He said something about being a fuck boy."

"What? What the hell does that mean?"

"It means he's there for you to fuck whenever you want."

I was basically done with this conversation. My brother was making it sound like what we'd been doing was somehow cheap or disgusting and I was not going to be slut shamed by my own brother. "Steven, listen to me. Your sex life is your own business. I don't ask and I don't care who was in your bed last night. I know this might seem weird to you because Maddox is your best friend, but he's my friend too, and friends can do whatever they want if everyone is on board with it, and it has absolutely nothing to do with you, so stay out of it."

"You're going to end up pregnant again and alone."

Tears stung my eyes and my lip started to tremble. My brother thought I was an idiot that no one could love. Wow.

I ended the call without a word. I was too hurt to find any words to express how I felt.

After crying for half an hour, I texted my co-worker Simone who had gone through a custody fight and asked for her lawyer's info so I could make an appointment to review the document from Adam.

Then I lay down on my bed with Sully and let him crawl all over me.

Talk about going from an all-time high the night before to so low I could win the limbo.

I GOT BACK to Brooklyn around eleven and as I walked from the bus to the apartment I texted Savannah. I didn't want to scare her when I came into the apartment since I wasn't supposed to be back until the next day.

Hey, be at the apt in 5. Don't want to scare you.

Thought you were coming back tomorrow?

I want to see you.

She didn't respond to that. I had no idea what that meant other than she might already be in bed and I was disturbing her sleep. Or it could mean she didn't want to see me.

The apartment was dark, so I reached over and turned on the lamp by the couch. The place was messier than usual. Savannah and Sully were clearly in bed because of how quiet the apartment was, but there were toys all over the floor and a plate on the coffee table, which wasn't typical. Savannah usually cleaned up at the end of the day. Meeting with her ex must have been emotionally draining.

I dropped my backpack and kicked off my shoes. I washed my hands and face in the bathroom, and shucked my shirt. I was planning to crawl into bed with her, figuring we'd reached that point, when she came out of the bedroom and pulled the door carefully shut behind her.

"Hey," she said, leaning on the bathroom doorframe in her baggy joggers and a T-shirt. Her hair was messy and her eyes were bloodshot, her face swollen.

I had a sneaking suspicion she'd been crying.

"Are you okay?" I asked, going to her and pulling her against me. She didn't wrap her arms around me but let me hold her. "Isla told me your ex showed up here. I'm sorry you had to deal with that alone. If you want me to track him down and punch him, I will." I was only half kidding.

Her fingers were flat against my chest. She sighed. "Not worth risking assault charges. It wasn't fun but it wasn't horrible either. He's just such an ass and I feel terrible that he doesn't want Sully at all. He wants to sign away his parental rights."

My reaction was probably wrong, but I was relieved. "How do you feel about that?"

"I don't want him showing up at random intervals, so I guess in the end this is best, but I still feel sad for my son. It's not fair that my poor choices mean he won't have a father."

I stroked her arms. "Savannah, it's not your fault. It's your ex's fault. You couldn't have predicted his reaction to finding out you were pregnant. Some guys can man up, others can't."

She sniffled. "You and me… this is a bad idea, Maddox."

I stiffened and pulled back to study her face. She had tears in her eyes. "What are you talking about? Is this because of your brother? I'm sorry, I didn't mean for him to find out but I was talking to Isla when she called me about your ex and he overheard the conversation."

"Steven called me. He's pissed at both of us. You for taking advantage of me and me for being stupid enough to fall for it." She shook her head and her voice trembled. "That's how highly my brother thinks of both of us, which is insulting. No, I'm not worried about Steven's opinion right now."

"Then what is it?" I took her hand. "Come here. Let's sit down. We don't want to have this conversation in the bathroom."

My gut was tight and I was trying to stay calm, rational. Talk her down off whatever ledge she'd climbed onto as a result of her ex and her brother. She'd been all on board the night before.

We sat down and she pulled her legs under her.

"I agree that we could have talked more about what was happening, what this means," I said. "Because just to be clear, what I want is you. I'm in love with you and I want to be with you, in a relationship. Indefinitely. I love Sully and I will treat him like my own flesh and blood. I have a good example in my own stepfather and I know I'm capable of that." I took her hand and kissed the back of it. "I love you, Savannah."

The tears slid down her cheeks. "I believe you. I believe you mean that. Now. But what happens in a year when all your friends are out partying and you're stuck at home with a girlfriend and a toddler?"

That took me aback. "What are you talking about? When did I ever say I wanted to party? Do you see me partying now?"

"Because you've been obligated to help me out."

I was starting to shift from puzzled to pissed. "Why is this coming up now? That was never a big deal between us. You never once asked me if I felt stuck at home. I told you my goal was to go home, to be near my family. I told you I'm not a guy who fucks every girl who gives him a smile. That's your brother, not me. And you knew that."

She bit her lip. "I can't make a mistake, Maddox. Not another one. Look where I'm at because I'm romantic and gullible and believe everything men tell me. Being served parental rights termination papers."

I was pretty sure I'd never understood the phrase "saw red" until Savannah spoke those words. "I'm not *men.* I'm not your asshole ex. I'm me. Maddox. The man who has loved you since he was still a kid."

"Exactly," she said, and her voice was pleading. "I'm just a fantasy to you."

She had just hit my second hot button. I stood up, unable to sit. I put my hands behind my head to try to cool down. I took a deep breath and said very calmly, "Do not tell me how I feel or what you are to me. I know my own emotions. This, what we've been doing for weeks and weeks is not a fantasy. It's real and you know it."

Now she was full-on crying. "I just can't trust that this is right. I can't risk this. If it goes wrong, it's on me that I did this to Sully twice, and this time it will be worse, because he knows you and cares about you." She swiped at her face. "I need to take more time, date with more distance."

For a second, I felt a flicker of hope. "Okay. You want me to move out, not spend so much time with Sully. I get that. We can do that. It's not what I want, but I can respect that. Maybe we did this all backward."

But she shook her head. "No, that's not what I mean. I meant in the future, when I'm dating…"

Someone else. Those were the unspoken words.

Fuck. Fuck and fuck.

"I fall in love too easily," she finished.

Damn.

I wasn't anything special. That's what she was saying.

I thought for a second, and decided I had nothing to lose. I'd already given her my heart and she was handing it back. "I know I don't fit in with your ideal, what you pictured for your life. I don't have a job on Wall Street and a yacht and I am only twenty-four and covered in tattoos. This is me. This ink isn't erasable. And maybe that's embarrassing for a woman like you to have to explain on the playground to the other moms, I don't know. And I'm not going to toss rose petals across the bedroom floor or take you on a carriage ride like the dudes in your movies.

I tried to be Ryan Reynolds and I don't think it's a good fit for me."

"What are you talking about? And I'm not embarrassed of you. Why would you even think that?"

"I tried to listen to Jana. She had me watching rom-coms and trying to figure out how I could take you ice-skating and all these other crazy schemes so you fall in love with me."

"*That's* why you wanted to go ice-skating?" she asked, looking stunned. "I just thought you wanted fresh air."

I might have laughed at that except my heart felt like it was caught in a garbage compactor. We were getting off track.

"You said it yourself. I'm not romantic. I did come here with an agenda of being with you, I can admit that. Sure, it was for the show. But it was also for *you*. And maybe I suck at being the wine and dine guy. Maybe I won't take you to some fancy-ass restaurant or throw you a circus engagement party. But do you know what I will do? I will be there for you every single fucking day, and I will respect you, and take care of you and love you with all my heart. I will help you raise your son and I'll give you another one if that's what you want. I *stick*, Savannah."

There it was. My whole fucking heart on a platter handed over to her.

I stood there, waiting, feeling like my future, my everything, rested on her next words.

She was crying, her knees drawn up to her chest. "I… I don't know what to do."

There it was. Like a punch in the gut.

She wasn't ready to commit to me.

Or maybe she just didn't want me.

Maybe I'd been companionship. An orgasm. A friend, nothing more.

My jaw worked. I bent over and grabbed my backpack. "I'll sleep at Jana's tonight. I'll come by tomorrow to get the rest of my stuff."

"Mad, wait…" She tried to stand up, but her feet were tangled in her blanket.

But I couldn't stick around. "It's fine, Savannah. I'll be fine. I hope you find what you're looking for some day, I really do. And I hope you'll let me say goodbye to Sully tomorrow. I really do love him."

My throat constricted and I just shook my head. I had nothing left to say. I took three steps and made it to the door. I ran down the stairs, my boots pounding the concrete. I burst onto the street and looked up at the sky.

No stars.

It was all so fucking unfair.

Chapter 16

I ALMOST FELL face-first onto the floor scrambling to get off of the couch. "Maddox!"

The door slammed shut behind him.

Where the hell were my keys? And my shoes? I needed to go after him but I couldn't go far because of Sully. Just downstairs. But if I caught him in front of the building, it would be okay.

By the time I found my keys and grabbed my phone, it was too late to worry about shoes, so I locked my apartment door behind me and ran down the stairs in socks. I shoved open the front door of my building and slid outside a la Bridget Jones, though wearing pants.

"Maddox!"

I didn't see him in either direction.

"Shit!" He was just gone.

I had things to say to him. I needed to explain myself better. That I was trying to do the right thing, that I didn't want to hurt him. Most of all, that I did love him. That I didn't care about tattoos (hell, those were hot) but I didn't trust myself. I hadn't said any of it right.

I called him but he didn't pick up. I jumped up and down in frustration, making tight fists. "Argh!"

Then I went back upstairs because I wasn't going to leave

Sully alone for longer than a minute or two. I called Maddox again. This time it went right to voicemail. He'd either turned off his phone or declined my call.

I thought about texting him but I wasn't sure what to say.

He had said he would return the next day for his stuff. That would give me at least ten hours to figure out what to say.

I threw myself on my bed facedown and marveled at the irony that the night before I had been in this same position and Maddox had been lying next to me. Now I was alone and frankly, I deserved it.

I stayed up half the night, tossing and turning, tearing up, berating myself and life and all things Julia Roberts.

Around four, I finally fell asleep and dreamed that Ryan Reynolds was in my face, laughing hysterically.

MY HEAD WAS POUNDING like I'd downed four martinis, but I dragged myself into the shower and got both myself and Sully ready. The girls and I had brunch plans. Dakota liked to call us the bitches who brunch, but I liked to think of it more as #squad-goals. We tried to make time every couple of months to do brunch, and thank all the powers of the universe it was brunch Sunday because I needed serious advice.

Dakota stared at me over her chicken and waffles. "I'm so confused."

We had spent the first twenty minutes of brunch going over Leah's amazing engagement party, catching up on each other's Instagram stories from the event, and complimenting Leah on how beautiful she had looked. Which was exactly the way it should be two days after your engagement party. But when the conversation had drifted to Dakota's upcoming laser hair removal I figured I could explain what had gone down between me and Maddox.

"Well, that makes two of us," I said, aggressively wiping down the tray and area in front of Sully with an antibacterial wipe for the second time.

"Friday night he tells you he loves you. You say it back. Am I right? And now he's moving out and you are basically breaking up?" She turned to Isla. "Does that make sense to you?"

"I'm picking through it." Isla lifted up her coffee, and set it back down. "Nope. I'm in the dark."

"What is there to explain?" I said, feeling exasperated. "He basically told me he came here with a crush still and that he planned to have sex with me. It wasn't totally spontaneous. I told him that I can't be trusted to make good decisions when it comes to men and now that I have a son I need to be…" I was searching for the right word.

"Celibate?" Felicia asked.

"Ew. That wasn't exactly what I meant, but I guess so, yes."

"When is sex ever actually spontaneous?" Leah asked. "I could sit here and argue that the first time Grant and I hooked up was spontaneous. Twisted ankle, a ride home, etc. But that only happened because we'd been lusting after each other for six months. You were lusting after Maddox since the second you saw him and apparently, he's been lusting after you for a decade." She sipped her mimosa, clearly a woman who knew things now that she was engaged.

"Ugh, this is such a mess. My brother was a complete ass about the whole thing. He told me I was going to end up pregnant and lonely for the second time."

"What the hell?" Dakota's jaw dropped. "I think your brother needs his butt beat."

"Agreed. I haven't even heard from him since I hung up on him."

"Do we still hang up on people?" Felicia asked. "Or do we end the call? That sounds so unwieldy."

"Focus," I said, through gritted teeth. "Tell me what I'm supposed to do now."

"I guess nothing," Isla said, giving a casual shrug. "You've already figured it all out."

I stared her down. "Don't do that."

"Do what?" she asked, tilting her head. "Tell me, Savannah. What am I doing?"

"Refusing to indulge me."

"Because you're not telling us the truth of it. What are you afraid of?"

"I did tell you." I was frustrated and kept checking at my phone. Nothing from Maddox. "I'm afraid of Sully getting hurt."

"And?"

I swallowed. "I'm afraid of me getting hurt. I'm afraid that Maddox will get older and decide that he doesn't want me."

"It's okay to be afraid of those things," Felicia said, reaching for my hand. "Most people are afraid to be rejected and abandoned. If they're not, they're Isla."

That made me laugh, though it was a little wobbly.

"Newsflash," Isla said. "I act tough and defensive and don't date because I am afraid of being rejected. I don't need Freud to tell me that."

"What have you always wanted?" Leah asked me. "A forever guy, right? That has driven you in your dating since I've known you. You don't want to play the field and you're not afraid of commitment. Maddox is offering you all of that and if you don't at least try, I think you're nuts. You might as well delete all rom-coms from your streaming library."

The thought was horrifying. "I can't do that. Maddox told me he has been watching rom coms with Jana to try to do romantic things for me."

"That's fucking romantic," Dakota said. "In and of itself."

It was. I tucked my hair behind my ear. "I'm a mess."

My phone buzzed. It was Maddox.

At the apartment getting my stuff. Are you coming back soon?

I just sat down to brunch. Our food isn't here yet.

Okay. I'll get you your key another day.

No. That wasn't right.

You don't even want to talk?

What is there left to say?

Nothing. Everything. I read the texts out loud to my friends.

"What should I do?" I couldn't let him walk away like that. It was wrong. All wrong.

"This is real life," Isla said. "Unless you have something different to say, he's right. There isn't anything left to talk about."

That answer officially sucked.

I thought about Maddox on the fire escape. I thought about the look in his eyes when he had told me he loved me. The gentleness of his kiss. The steadiness of his friendship. The intensity of his passion.

"Or you follow the lead of your greatest heroines and take a leap of faith and go for it," Leah said. "You can take a risk, go after him, and be vulnerable."

"You're starring in your own movie," Dakota said. "Write the ending however you want."

All of us turned and gawked at Dakota.

"What?" she asked, sipping her bloody Mary. "It's true."

"I just never expected something so profound to emerge from you," Felicia said. "No offense."

"None taken." Dakota cheerfully dunked her celery in her drink.

She might as well have tossed that drink in my face. That was the effect her words had on me.

There was no way I could let my relationship with Maddox end like this.

He was the total package and I would be too stupid to live if I let fear prevent me from accepting what he was offering.

"Oh my God," I said, shoving my chair back. "I love him. I absolutely love him and I have to go find him." I was scrambling for my purse to pay for my brunch that hadn't even arrived yet.

"Don't worry about your food," Isla said. "I'll cancel your order."

I tried to unbuckle Sully but my fingers were trembling.

"Leave the baby," Felicia said. "We've got this. Just leave the diaper bag and his bottle. Go get your man."

"Are you sure?" I asked, heart pounding as I pulled on my coat.

"Absolutely. Now go. Seriously, run."

"Thank you!" I kissed Sully and blew them all a kiss and ran for the door. I was wearing boots with a heel which wasn't the best for a jog down the sidewalk but I threw my purse over my shoulder and went for it.

By the third block on my way to my apartment it was raining. The plan was to get to my apartment and stop Maddox before he left. It was a fifteen-minute walk but I managed it in under ten. I took the stairs, out of breath, and held on to the railing. My hair was damp and stuck to my forehead.

Fumbling with my key, I tumbled into the apartment. "Maddox!"

It was obvious almost immediately he wasn't there. The apartment was still and there was no sign of him. His suitcase in the corner was gone. "Damn it!" I kicked the couch and then jumped up and down. "Ow, fuck. That hurt."

I went into the bathroom as I pulled my phone out. I texted Maddox.

Where are you?

Almost to the train station. Going back to Jana's until I figure out where I'm living.

Don't get on the train. Wait for me.

He didn't answer, which wasn't promising. I didn't even know where Jana lived, so I wasn't sure what line he would take.

But I would be a fool not to at least try.

I locked my apartment behind me and took off running again. Or maybe not running. More like jogging breathlessly. The rain had ramped up and by the time I got to the subway I was absolutely drenched, hanks of heavy hair plastered to my head and face. The front of my pants were wet to the knee from plowing through puddles.

Swiping my card, I tried to go through the turnstile too fast and nearly knocked myself out bouncing off the barrier. Once I was through, I took off for the platform, dodging a guy playing the trumpet. I kept jumping up and down as I was running to see if I could catch a glimpse of Maddox over the other heads. He was a tall guy. I might be able to scan and spot him.

I did the world's fastest social media dive into Jana, finding her on the tattoo shop's website to figure out her last name and then going to her various accounts. She lived in Harlem from what I could tell.

C train. I was on the right track. The train was arriving.

Suddenly, I saw him. He was standing back from the train, backpack on, suitcase next to him. He looked angry and sad.

And gorgeous. God, he was just the hottest man ever.

"Maddox!" I yelled, as I maneuvered around an elderly woman with a cane, trying my hardest not to jostle her. "Maddox!"

He turned.

We locked eyes.

I was five feet away and it might as well have been a hundred. Every step was agony as he watched me, jaw set.

When I finally reached him, I just stood there for a second trying to regain my breath. I was panting and had a stitch in my side. I bent over slightly and held my finger up to indicate I needed a second. Why did that never happen to the star in movies? I was eating a lung.

"Savannah, what are you doing?" he asked.

I stood back up and pushed my wet hair back, shivering. "I love you," I said, because that seemed like a good lead in and I didn't have a better one. I just needed to spill my guts. "I love you and I don't want you to go. I'm sorry I panicked but I want to be with you, for now, for forever."

His reaction wasn't quite what I expected. His nostrils flared but he just asked, "Why? What is different from last night?"

My assumption had been he would just open his arms and accept me. He was a tough audience and it was clear I'd really hurt him. I needed to make this super clear. I scrambled for the right words.

"I started thinking about you and what you said—that I don't get to tell you how you feel. You're right. That wasn't fair to you. You know what else? Your producer was wrong. You are actually the most romantic man I've ever met."

That got a reaction. He scoffed a little.

But I continued on, dogged and determined. "Rooftop dinners are for guys out to impress. You know what's romantic? Getting up at 3 a.m. to help me with a crying baby that isn't yours. Romantic is making me a cauliflower pizza that you think smells like socks. Romantic is having silent sex so we don't wake the baby. It's dancing with me at Chelsea Pier with your suit jacket wrapped around me because I have stains on my dress." I splayed my hands across his strong chest. "It's your amazing ability to always put me and Sully ahead of yourself and how you stay calm and reassuring when I'm neurotic. That's romantic, Maddox Malone. You can't tell me otherwise."

He was softening. He touched my hair, my cheek. "Why do you look like you've fallen in the river?" he murmured.

"It's pouring." I was wet and my clothes were uncomfortable and I was cold but I wasn't leaving until he gave me some kind of answer. "And I ran twenty blocks to tell you that I love you and you've said exactly nothing about that."

Drastic action was required. I always talked about a grand gesture. Time to stand by my convictions. Wobbling a little, I went down on a knee and took his hand. "Will you be my fifth first date?"

His jaw worked. "Savannah. Get off the floor." He tugged my hand, and pulled me up. He cupped my cheeks and kissed me, a sweet, yet sensual kiss. "I love you too," he said. "I will be your fifth and *final* first date. I am one hundred percent in. Forever."

Relief and happiness flooded through me.

"That was always my plan, you know," he said. "When I said I was picking out a fifth date for you I always meant it to be me."

"So much for friends with benefits," I said, gleefully, throwing my arms around his neck. "Whoops."

"Now let's really give you the ending you want," he said.

I let out a startled laugh when he wrapped an arm under my butt and lifted me up. I found myself tossed over his shoulder. He held me with exactly zero effort on his part like I weighed nothing. I shrieked and held on for dear life, loving every single second of it.

"I'm taking you home." Maddox carried me down the platform. "Roll the credits."

Giddy, bouncing on him, I looked around me at everyone. A few people were watching, most looked unconcerned or disinterested. I couldn't have cared less what anyone thought.

I'd gotten my perfect happily ever after and I was never letting it go.

Epilogue

"Jana sent me the link," I told Savannah as we stood on the platform overlooking the skating rink. "Let's look at it together." I held my phone in front of us and made the video bigger. Then I hit play.

It was the trailer for Rebel Ink, which was due to debut in April.

The music was pounding and rapid, which quick shots of the shop, then they showed Travis doing a tattoo, then Jana and Stella snarking at each other. Samuel and Stella yelling. They'd clearly gone for the drama. Maybe I was on the cutting room floor. That kind of sucked.

But then there was a shot of me and Savannah sitting next to each other.

"Who doesn't love a hot guy with some great tats?" she said.

Then it ended with the date it was being dropped, eight episodes available all at once to binge watch. I wasn't exactly the star of that trailer, but I could have cared less.

"Wow, that's so good!" she said, trying for perky. "This is exciting!"

She almost convinced me. Savannah was the world's best cheerleader.

"That clip of me is ridiculous," I said. "But I honestly don't care. Filming a second season already is making it a hell of a lot easier to stay here." I would have found a way no matter what, but having a steady job helped.

"I'm so proud of you," she said.

I stuck my phone back in my pocket and smiled at her. "Thanks for going ice skating with me."

It was almost Valentine's Day. We hadn't made it skating before Jana's deadline but hey, at least I'd gotten her there.

"Unlike when I was a bitchy teen, I am planning to have fun." She smiled at me. "Because you make me so very, very happy."

"I feel the same way."

My sister Kyle popped up between us. "Are we skating? Are we skating?"

Savannah laughed. "Yes, we are." She put her hand on Kyle's head and gave me an amused smile. "I'm so happy our families are here for the weekend."

I nodded. She had no idea.

Her parents had been a little startled but actually thrilled with our relationship. I'd spent so much time with them over the years they were very confident in my character. Her mother had cried and her father had choked up when I'd asked him permission to marry Savannah.

Steve hadn't been as thrilled, but he was getting over it. He just didn't want details about our relationship and that was fair.

My family was ecstatic. Everyone liked Savannah and my parents didn't think I needed to spend the next ten years screwing around. They knew that wasn't my personality. They were over by the concession area with her parents and Sully.

I held my hand out for Savannah and we stepped into the rink as Kyle ran back to my parents.

Savannah wobbled a little and laughed but then found her footing. Then she stopped. "Wait, is that Mark? Over there?" She pointed to her right. She waved.

Shit. He and the crew were not supposed to be visible.

Mark pretended like he didn't see her.

"We should go hi," she said, because that was Savannah.

I held her back when she would have skated off in that direction. "Maybe in a minute. First, I want to ask you something."

She turned back. "What?"

Something on my face must have given it away because her mouth dropped open. "Mad…"

Going down on one knee on the ice I pulled the ring box out and lifted the lid. "Savannah, I told you forever and I meant that. I know it's soon, but I don't see any reason to wait when we both know that we're best friends who can trust each other. You're my everything and I am never going to let you go. Will you be my wife?"

She nodded. "Yes! Are you kidding? Yes!" She bounced up and down in excitement.

I knew a grand gesture would get her.

I realized about a heartbeat too late though she was going down from her enthusiasm on skates. I couldn't have stopped her fall anyway since I was on one knee. She screamed and I shifted so that she would land on me instead of the ice. Her elbow went straight into my gut.

"You meant to do that," I told her. "Right?"

Savannah laughed breathlessly. "Exactly."

We kissed, and I breathed in the crisp cold air and what it felt like to be in love with Savannah and about to be her husband.

"Did she say yes?" a loud voice called from the side of the rink.

It was Steve, looking begrudgingly happy for us.

"Yes. She said yes."

Our families standing together erupted into cheers and applause.

"Was this Jana's idea?" Savannah laughed, when we saw her suddenly jump out from behind a couple.

Jana was jumping up and down and cheering. I'd had to let her be a part of the proposal given how invested she'd been from day one in our relationship.

"No. This was all me. And for the record, the fire escape was all me too."

She threw her arms around me. We were surrounded by tons of people and yet it felt like no one else existed but the two of us.

"That's because you're Mr. Romance."

"Don't ever call me that again," I said wryly.

"Maddy?" she teased.

"Stop."

"Number five?"

Now she was really enjoying herself. "You're getting colder."

"Prince Charming?"

I grimaced. "Anything but that."

Savannah gave me a smile and a kiss. "I think I'll just call you mine. Now get me off this ice."

Thank you for reading Five First Dates!

Weekend Wife

Billionaire businessman in need of a fake fiancée...

It should be the easiest job ever for an out-of-work actress, right?

All I have to do is pose as Grant Caldwell (the Third)'s fiancée for a fancy-pants weekend in the Hamptons. Easy. Wear designer clothing and sip champagne? Don't mind if I do. Flirting with Grant? It's so delicious I should be paying *him*.

Nothing can go wrong as long as I can just keep my hands off of him.

But that's the hard part. And I do mean *hard*.

Because Grant is sexy.
And bossy.
And surprisingly sweet, a real rarity in his pretentious family.

Oops. I'm not as good at faking it as I thought. Or maybe they call this method acting. Because it's getting harder to figure out where my character ends and I begin…

It just might be the role of a lifetime.

About the Author

USA Today and New York Times Bestselling author Erin McCarthy sold her first book in 2002 and has since written almost eighty novels and novellas in the romance and mystery genres. Erin has a special weakness for tattoos, high-heeled boots, and martinis. She lives with her renovation-addicted husband and their blended family of kids and rescue dogs.

Also by Erin McCarthy

TAP THAT Series

Read Stripped Down

When Sloane returns to her old hometown, she reunites with her younger brother's best friend, Rick — while he's stripping at a charity event! Will they relive their forbidden kiss… and maybe explore their tension in the bedroom? A sizzling romantic comedy!

Strip Search

Strip Tease

Made in the USA
Las Vegas, NV
08 June 2021

24391268R00121